Under the S

Under the Storm

Charlotte M. Yonge

Vij Books India Pvt Ltd
New Delhi (India)

Published by

Vij Books India Pvt Ltd
(Publishers, Distributors & Importers)
2/19, Ansari Road
Delhi – 110 002
Phones: 91-11-43596460, Mob: 98110 94883
e-mail: contact@vijpublishing.com
web: www.vijbooks.in

Copyright © 2023

ISBN: 978-93-95675-48-2

Contents

CHAPTER I

THE TRUST

"I brought them here as to a sanctuary."
SOUTHEY.

Most of us have heard of the sad times in the middle of the seventeenth century, when Englishmen were at war with one another and quiet villages became battlefields.

We hear a great deal about King and Parliament, great lords and able generals, Cavaliers and Roundheads, but this story is to help us to think how it must have gone in those times with quiet folk in cottages and farmhouses.

There had been peace in England for a great many years, ever since the end of the wars of the Roses. So the towns did not want fortifications to keep out the enemy, and their houses spread out beyond the old walls; and the country houses had windows and doors large and wide open, with no thought of keeping out foes, and farms and cottages were freely spread about everywhere, with their fields round them.

The farms were very small, mostly held by men who did all the work themselves with the help of their families.

Such a farm belonged to John Kenton of Elmwood. It lay at the head of a long green lane, where the bushes overhead almost touched one another in the summer, and the mud and mire were very deep in winter; but that mattered the less as nothing on wheels went up or down it but the hay or harvest carts, creaking under their load, and drawn by the old mare, with a cow to help her.

Beyond lay a few small fields, and then a bit of open ground scattered with gorse and thorn bushes, and much broken by ups and downs. There, one afternoon on a big stone was seated Steadfast Kenton, a boy of fourteen, sturdy, perhaps loutish, with an honest ruddy face under his leathern cap, a coarse smock frock and stout gaiters. He was watching the fifteen sheep and lambs, the old goose and gander and their nine children, the three cows, eight pigs, and the old donkey which got their living there.

From the top of the hill, beyond the cleft of the river Avon, he could see the smoke and the church towers of the town of Bristol, and beyond it, the slime of the water of the Bristol Channel; and nearer, on one side, the spire of Elmwood Church looked up, and, on the other, the woods round Elmwood House, and these ran out as it were, lengthening and narrowing into a wooded cleft or gulley, Hermit's Gulley, which broke the side of the hill just below where Steadfast stood, and had a little clear stream running along the bottom.

Steadfast's little herd knew the time of day as well as if they all had watches in their pockets, and they never failed to go down and have a drink at the brook before going back to the farmyard.

They did not need to be driven, but gathered into the rude steep path that they and their kind had worn in the side of the ravine. Steadfast followed, looking about him to judge how soon the nuts would be ripe, while his little rough stiff-haired dog Toby poked about in search of rabbits or hedgehogs, or the like sport.

Steadfast liked that pathway home beside the stream, as boys do love running water. Good stones could be got there, water rats might be chased, there were strawberries on the banks which he gathered and threaded on stalks of grass for his sisters, Patience and Jerusha. They used to come with him and have pleasant games, but it was a long time since Patience had been able to come out, for in the winter, a grievous trouble had come on the family. The good mother had died, leaving a little baby of six weeks old, and Patience, who was only thirteen, had to attend to everything at home, and take care of poor little sickly Benoni with no one to help her but her little seven years old sister.

The children's lives had been much less bright since that sad day; and Steadfast seldom had much time for play. He knew he must get home as fast as he could to help Patience in milking the cows, feeding the pigs and poultry, and getting the supper, or some of the other things that his elder brother Jephthah called wench-work and would not do.

He could not, however, help looking up at the hole in the side of the steep cliff, where one might climb up to such a delightful cave, in which he and Patience had so often played on hot days. It had been their secret, and a kind of palace to them. They had sat there as king and queen, had paved it with stones from the brook, and had had many plans for the sports they would have there this summer, little thinking that Patience would have been turned into a grave, busy little housewife, instead of a merry, playful child.

Toby looked up too, and began to bark. There was a rustling in the bushes below the cave, and Steadfast, at first in dismay to see his secret delight invaded, beheld between the mountain ash boughs and ivy, to his great surprise, a square cap and black cassock tucked up, and then a bit of brown leathern coat, which he knew full well. It was the Vicar, Master Holworth, and his father John Kenton was Churchwarden, so it was no wonder to see him and the Parson together, but what could bring them here—into Steadfast's cave? and with a dark lantern too! They seemed as surprised, perhaps as vexed as he was, at the sight of him, but his father said, "'Tis my lad, Steadfast, I'll answer for him."

"And so will I," returned the clergyman. "Is anyone with you, my boy?"

"No, your reverence, no one save the beasts."

"Then come up here," said his father. "Someone has been playing here, I see."

"Patience and I, father, last summer."

"No one else?"

"No, no one. We put those stones and those sticks when we made a fire there last year, and no one has meddled with them since."

"Thou and Patience," said Mr. Holworth thoughtfully. "Not Jephthah nor the little maid?"

"No, sir," replied Steadfast, "we would not let them know, because we wanted a place to ourselves."

For in truth the quiet ways and little arrangements of these two had often been much disturbed by the rough elder brother who teased and laughed at them, and by the troublesome little sister, who put her fingers into everything.

The Vicar and the Churchwarden looked at one another, and John Kenton muttered, "True as steel."

"Your father answers for you, my boy," said the Vicar. "So we will e'en let you know what we are about. I was told this morn by a sure hand that the Parliament men, who now hold Bristol Castle, are coming to deal with the village churches even as they have dealt with the minster and with St. Mary's, Redcliffe."

"A murrain on them!" muttered Kenton.

"I wot that in their ignorance they do it," gently quoted the Vicar. "But we would fain save from their hands the holy Chalice and paten which came down to our Church from the ancient times—and which bearing on them, as they do, the figure of the Crucifixion of our blessed Lord, would assuredly provoke the zeal of the destroyers. Therefore have we placed them in this casket, and your father devised hiding them within this cave, which he thought was unknown to any save himself—"

"Yea," said John, "my poor brother Will and I were wont to play there when we herded the cattle on the hill. It was climbing yon ash tree that stands out above that he got the fall that was the death of him at last. I've never gone nigh the place with mine own good will since that day—nor knew the children had done so—but methought 'twas a lonesome place and on mine own land, where we might safest store the holy things till better times come round."

"And so I hope they will," said Mr. Holworth.

"I hear good news of the King's cause in the north."

Then they began to consult where to place the precious casket. They had brought tinder and matches, and Steadfast, who knew the secrets of the cave even better than his father, showed them a little hollow, far back, which would just hold the chest, and being closed in front with a big stone, fast wedged in, was never likely to be discovered readily.

"This has been a hiding place already."

"Methinks this has once been a chapel," said the clergyman presently, pointing to some rude carvings—one something like a cross, and a large stone that might have served as an altar.

"Belike," said Kenton, "there's an old stone pile, a mere hovel, down below, where my grandfather said he remembered an old monk, a hermit, or some such gear—a Papist—as lived in hiding. He did no hurt, and was a man from these parts, so none meddled with him, or gave notice to the Queen's officers, and our folk at the farm sold his baskets at the town, and brought him a barley loaf twice a week till he died, all alone in his hut. Very like he said his mass here."

John wondered to find that the minister thought this made the place more suitable. The whole cavern was so low that the two men could hardly stand upright in it, though it ran about twelve yards back. There were white limestone drops like icicles hanging above from the roof; and bats, disturbed by the light, came flying about the heads of their visitors, while streamers of ivy and old man's beard hung over the mouth, and were displaced by the heads of the men.

"None is like to find the spot," said John Kenton, as he tried to replace the tangled branches that had been pushed aside.

"God grant us happier days for bringing it forth," said the clergyman.

All three bared their heads, and Mr. Holworth uttered a few words of prayer and blessing; then let John help him down the steep scramble and descent, and looked up to see whether any sign of the cave could be detected from the edge of the brook. Kenton shook his head reassuringly.

"Ah!" said Mr. Holworth, "it minds me that none ever found again the holy Ark of the Covenant that King Josiah and the Prophet Jeremiah hid in a cavern within Mount Pisgah! and our sins be many that have provoked this judgment! Mayhap the boy will be the only one of us who will see these blessed vessels restored to their Altar once more! He may have been sent hither to that very end. Now, look you, Steadfast Kenton—Steadfast thou hast ever been, so far as I have known thee, in nature as well as in name. Give me thy word that thou wilt never give up the secret of yonder cavern to any save a lawfully ordained minister of the church."

"No doubt poor old Clerk North will be in distress about the loss," said Kenton.

"True, but he had best not be told. His mind is fast going, and he cannot safely be trusted with such a mighty secret."

"Patience knows the cavern," murmured Steadfast to his father.

"Best have no womenfolk, nor young maids in such a matter," said the Vicar.

"My wench takes after her good mother," said John, "and I ever found my secrets were safer in her breast than in mine own. Not that I would have her told without need. But she might take little Rusha there, or make the place known to others an she be not warned."

"Steadfast must do as he sees occasion, with your counsel, Master Kenton," said the Vicar. "It is a great trust we place in you, my son, to be as it were in charge of the vessels of the sanctuary, and I would have thy hand and word."

"And," said his father, "though he be slower in speech than some, your reverence may trust him."

Steadfast gave his brown red hand, and with head bare said, "I promise, after the minister and before God, never to give up that which lies within the cave to any man, save a lawfully ordained minister of the Church."

CHAPTER II

THE STRAGGLERS

"Trust me, I am exceedingly weary."
SHAKESPEARE.

John Kenton, though a Churchwarden, was, as has been said, a very small farmer, and the homestead was no more than a substantial cottage, built of the greystone of the country, with the upper story projecting a little, and reached by an outside stair of stone. The farm yard, with the cowsheds, barn, and hay stack were close in front, with only a narrow strip of garden between, for there was not much heed paid to flowers, and few kitchen vegetables were grown in those days, only a few potherbs round the door, and a sweet-brier bush by the window.

The cows had made their way home of their own accord, and Patience was milking one of them already, while little Rusha held the baby, which was swaddled up as tightly as a mummy, with only his arms free. He stretched them out with a cry of gladness as he saw his father, and Kenton took the little creature tenderly in his arms and held him up, while Steadfast hurried off to fetch the milking stool and begin upon the other cow.

"Is Jeph come home?" asked the father, and Rusha answered "No, daddy, though he went ever so long ago, and said he would bring me a cake."

Upon this Master Kenton handed little Benoni back to Rusha, not without some sounds of fretfulness from the baby, but the pigs had to be shut up and fed, and the other evening work of the farmyard done; and it was not till all this was over, and Patience had disposed of the milk in the cool cellars, that the father could take him again.

Meantime Steadfast had brought up a bucket of water from the spring, and after washing his own hands and face, set out the table with a very clean, though coarse cloth, five brown bowls, three horn spoons and two wooden ones, one drinking horn, a couple of red earthen cups and two small hooped ones of wood, a brown pitcher of small ale, a big barley loaf, and a red crock, lined with yellow glazing, into which Patience presently proceeded to pour from a cauldron, where it had been simmering over the fire, a mess of broth thickened with meal. This does not sound like good living, but the Kentons were fairly well-to-do smock-frock farmers, and though in some houses there might be greater plenty, there was not much more comfort beneath the ranks of the gentry in the country.

As for seats, the father's big wooden chair stood by the fire, and there was a long settle, but only stools were used at the table, two being the same that had served the milkers. Just as Rusha, at her father's sign, had uttered a short Grace, there stood in the doorway a tall, stout, well-made lad of seventeen, with a high-crowned wide-brimmed felt hat, a dark jerkin with sleeves, that, like his breeches and gaiters, were of leather, and a belt across his shoulder with a knife stuck in it.

"Ha! Jeph," said Kenton, "always in time for meat, whatever else you miss."

"I could not help it, father," said Jephthah, "the red coats were at their exercise!"

"And thou couldst not get away from the gape-seed, eh! Come, sit down, boy, and have at thy supper."

"I wish I was one of them," said Jeph as he sat down.

"And thou'dst soon wish thyself back again!" returned his father.

"How much did you get for the fowls and eggs?" demanded Patience.

Jephthah replied by producing a leathern bag, while Rusha cried out for her cake, and from another pocket came, wrapped in his handkerchief, two or three saffron buns which were greeted with such joy that his father had not the heart to say much about wasting pence, though it appeared that the baker woman had given them as part of her bargain for a couple of dozen of eggs, which Patience declared ought to have brought two pence instead of only three halfpence.

Jephthah, however, had far too much news to tell to heed her disappointment as she counted the money. He declared that the price of eggs and butter would go up gallantly, for more soldiers were daily expected to defend Bristol, and he had further to tell of one of the captains preaching in the Minster, and the market people flocking in to hear him. Jeph had been outside, for there was no room within, but he had scrambled upon an old tombstone with a couple of other lads, and through the broken window had seen the gentleman holding forth in his hat and feather, buff coat and crimson scarf, and heard him call on all around to be strong and hew down all their enemies, even dragging the false and treacherous woman and her idols out to the horse gate and there smiting them even to the death.

"Who was the false woman?" asked Steadfast.

"I wot not! There was something about Aholah, or some such name, but just then a mischievous little jackanapes pulled me down by the leg, and I had to thrash him for it, and by the time I had done, Dick, the butcher's lad, had got my place and I heard no more."

Whether the Captain meant Aholah or Athaliah, or alluded to Queen Henrietta Maria, or to the English Church, Jeph's auditors never knew. The baby began to cry, and Patience to feed him with the milk and water that had been warmed at the fire; his father and the boys went out to finish the work for the night, little Rusha running after them.

Presently, she gave a cry and darted up to her father "The soldiers! the soldiers!" and in fact three men with steel caps, buff coats, and musquets slung by broad belts were coming into the yard.

Kenton took up his little girl in his arms and went forward to meet them, but he soon saw they did not look dangerous, they were dragging along as if very tired and footsore and as if their weapons were a heavy weight.

"It's the goodman," said the foremost, a red-faced, good-natured looking fellow more like a hostler than a soldier, "have you seen Captain Lundy's men pass this way?"

"Not I!" said Kenton, "we lie out of the high road, you see."

"But I saw them, a couple of hours agone, marching into Bristol," said Jephthah coming forward.

"There now," said the man, "we did but stop at the sign of the 'Crab' the drinking of a pottle, and to bathe Jack's foot near there, and we have never been able to catch them up again! How far off be Bristol?"

"A matter of four mile across the ferry. You may see it from the hill above."

He looked stout enough though he gave a heavy sigh of weariness, and the other two, who were mere youths, not much older than Jeph, seemed quite spent, and heard of the additional four miles with dismay.

"Heart alive, lads," said their comrade, "ye'll soon be in good quarters, and mayhap the goodman here will give you a drink to carry ye on a bit further for the Cause."

"You are welcome to a draught for civility's sake," said Kenton, making a sign to his sons, who ran off to the house, "but I'm a plain man, and know nought about the Cause."

"Well, Master," said the straggler, as he leant his back against the barn, and his two companions sat down on the ground in the shelter, "I have heard a lot about the Cause, but all I know is that my Lord of Essex sent to call out five-and-twenty men from our parish, and the squire, he was in a proper rage with being rated to pay ship money, so—as I had fallen out with my master, mine host of the 'Griffin,' more fool I—I went with the young gentleman, and a proper ass I was to do so."

"Father said 'twas rank popery railing in the Communion table, when it was so handy to sit on or to put one's hat on," added one of the youths looking up. "So he was willing for me to go, and I thought I'd like to see the world, but I'd fain be at home again."

"So would not I," muttered the other lad.

"No," said the ex-tapster humorously, "for thou knowst the stocks be gaping for thee, Dick."

By this time Jeph and Stead had returned with a jug of small beer, a horn cup, and three hunches of the barley loaf. The men ate and drank, and then the tapster returning hearty thanks, called the others on, observing that if they did not make the best speed, they might miss their billet, and have to sleep in the streets, if not become acquainted with the lash.

On then unwillingly they dragged, as if one foot would hardly come after the other.

"Poor lads!" said Kenton, as he looked after them, "methinks that's enough to take the taste for soldiering out of thy mouth, son Jeph."

"A set of poor-spirited rogues," returned Jeph contemptuously, as he nevertheless sauntered on so as to watch them down the lane.

"Be they on the right side or the wrong, father?" asked Steadfast, as he picked up the pitcher and the horn.

"They be dead against our parson, lad," returned Kenton, "and he says they be against the Church and the King, though they do take the King's name, it don't look like the right side to be knocking out church windows, eh?"

"Nay!" said Steadfast, "but there's them as says the windows be popish idols."

"Never you mind 'em, lad, ye don't bow down to the glass, nor worship it. Thy blessed mother would have put it to you better than I can, and she knew the Bible from end to end, but says she 'God would have His worship for glory and for beauty in the old times, why not now?'"

John Kenton had an immense reverence for his late wife. She had been far more educated than he, having been born and bred up in the household of one of those gentlemen who held it as their duty to provide for the religious instruction of their servants.

She had been serving-woman to the lady, who in widowhood went to reside at Bristol, and there during her marketings, honest John Kenton had won her by his sterling qualities.

Puritanism did not mean nonconformity in her days, and in fact everyone who was earnest and scrupulous was apt to be termed a Puritan. Goodwife

Kenton was one of those pious and simple souls who drink in whatever is good in their surroundings; and though the chaplain who had taught her in her youth would have differed in controversy with Mr. Holworth, she never discovered their diversity, nor saw more than that Elmwood Church had more decoration than the Castle Chapel. Whatever was done by authority she thought was right, and she found good reason for it in the Bible and Prayer-book her good lady had given her. She had named her children after the prevailing custom of Puritans because she had heard the chaplain object to what he considered unhallowed heathenish names, but she had been heartily glad that they should be taught and catechised by the good vicar. Happily for her, in her country home, she did not live to see the strife brought into her own life.

She had taught her children as much as she could. Her husband was willing, but his old mother disapproved of learning in that station of life, and aided and abetted her eldest grandson in his resistance, so that though she had died when he was only eleven or twelve years old, Jephthah could do no more than just make out the meaning of a printed sentence, whereas Steadfast and Patience could both read easily, and did read whatever came in their way, though that was only a broadside ballad now and then besides their mother's Bible and Prayer-book, and one or two little black books.

The three eldest had been confirmed, when the Bishop of Bath and Wells had been in the neighbourhood. That was only a fortnight after their mother died, and even Jeph was sad and subdued.

Since that sad day when the good mother had blessed them for the last time, there had been little time for anything. Patience had to be the busy little housewife, and what she would have done without Steadfast she could not tell. Jeph would never put a hand to what he called maids' work, but Stead would sweep, or beat the butter, or draw the water, or chop wood, or hold the baby, and was always ready to help her, even though it hindered him from ever going out to fish, or play at base ball, or any of the other sports the village boys loved.

His quiet, thoughtful ways had earned his father's trust, though he was much slower of speech and less ready than his elder brother, and looked heavy both in countenance and figure beside Jeph, who was tall, slim, and full of activity and animation. He had often made his mother uneasy by wild talk about going to sea, and by consorting with the sailors at Bristol, which was their nearest town, though on the other side of the Avon, and in a different county.

It was there that the Elmwood people did their marketing, often leaving their donkeys hobbled on their own side of the river, being ferried over and carrying the goods themselves the latter part of the way.

CHAPTER III

KIRK RAPINE

"When impious men held sway and wasted Church and shrine."
LORD SELBORNE.

Patience, in her tight little white cap, sat spinning by the door, rocking the cradle with her foot, while Rusha sometimes built what she called houses with stones, sometimes trotted to look down the lane to see whether father and the lads were coming home from market.

Presently she brought word, "Stead is coming. He is leading Whitefoot, but I don't see father and Jeph."

Patience jumped up to put her wheel out of the way, and soon she saw that it was only Steadfast leading the old mare with the large crooks or panniers on either side. She ran to meet him, and saw he looked rather pale and dazed.

"What is it, Stead? Where's daddy?"

"Gone up to Elmwood! They told us in town that some of the soldiers and the folk of that sort were gone out to rabble cur church and our parson, and father is Churchwarden, you know. So he said he must go to see what was doing. And he bade me take Whitefoot home and give you the money," said Steadfast, producing a bag which Patience took to keep for her father.

She watched very anxiously, and so did Stead, while relieving Whitefoot of her panniers and giving her a rub down before turning her out to get her supper.

It was not long however before Kenton and Jeph both appeared, the one looking sad, the other sulky. "Too late," Jeph muttered, "and father won't let me go to see the sport."

"Sport, d'ye call it?" said Kenton. "Aye, Stead, you may well gape at what we have seen—our good parson with his feet tied to his stirrups on a sorry nag, being hauled off to town like a common thief!"

"Oh!" broke from the children, and Patience ventured to ask, "But what for, father?"

"They best know who did it," said the Churchwarden. "Something they said of a scandalous minister, as though his had not ever been a godly life and preaching. These be strange times, children, and for the life of me, I know not what it all means. How now, Jeph, what art idling there for? There's the waggon to be loaded for to-morrow with the faggots I promised Mistress Lightfoot."

Jeph moved away, murmuring something about fetching up the cows, to which his father replied, "That was Steadfast's work, and it was not time yet."

In fact Jeph was very curious to know what was going on in the village. If there was any kind of uproar, why should not he have his part in it? It was just like father to hinder him, and he had a great mind to neglect the faggots and go off to the village. He was rather surprised, and a good deal vexed to see his father walking along on the way to the pasture with Steadfast.

It was for the sake of saying "Aye, boy, best not go near the sorry sight! They would not let good Master Holworth speak with me; but I saw he meant to warn me to keep aloof lest Tim Green or the like should remember as how I'm Churchwarden."

"Did they ask after those things?" inquired Steadfast in a lowered voice.

"I can't say. But on your life, lad, not a word of them!"

After work was done for the evening, Jeph and Stead were too eager to know what had happened to stay at home. They ran across the bit of moorland to the village street and the grey church, whose odd-shaped steeple stood up among the trees. Already they could see that the great west window was broken, all the glass which bore the picture of the Last Judgment, and the Archangel Michael weighing souls in the balance was gone!

"Yes," said Tom Oates, leaping over two or three tombstones to get to them. "'Twas rare sport, Jeph Kenton. Why were you not there too?"

"At Bristol with father," replied Jeph.

"Worse luck for you. The red coat shot the big angel right in the eye, and shivered him through, and we did the rest with stones. I sent one that knocked the wing of him right off. You should have seen me, Stead! And old Clerk North was running about crying all the time like a baby. He'll never whack us over the head again!"

"What was the good?" said Steadfast.

"You never saw better sport," said the boys.

And indeed, since, when once begun, destruction and mischief are apt to be only too delightful to boys, they had thoroughly and thoughtlessly delighted in knocking down the things they had been taught to respect. A figure of a knight in a ruff kneeling on a tomb had had its head knocked off, and one of the lads heaved the bits up to throw at the last fragment of glass in the window.

"What do you do that for?" asked Stead.

"'Tis worshipping of idols," said a somewhat graver lad. "'Break down their idols,' the man in the black gown said, 'and burn their graven images in the fire.'"

"But we never worshipped them," said Stead.

"Pious preacher said so," returned the youth, "and mighty angered was he with the rails." (Jeph and Will were sparring with two fragments of them.) "'Down with them,' he cried out, so as it would have done your heart good to hear him."

"And the parson is gone! There will be no hearing the catechism on Sundays!" cried Ralph Wilkes, making a leap over the broken font.

"Good luck for you, Ralph," cried the others. "You, that never could tell how many commandments there be."

"Put on your hat, Stead," called out another lad. "We've done with all that now, and the parson is gone to prison for it."

"No, no," shouted Tom Oates, "'twas for making away with the Communion things."

"I heard the red coat say they had a warrant against scandalous ministers," declared Ralph Wilkes.

"I heard the man with the pen and ink-horn ask for the popish vessels, as he called them, and not a word would the parson say," said Oates.

"I'd take my oath he has hid them somewheres," replied Jack Beard, an ill-looking lad.

"What a windfall they would be for him as found them!" observed Wilkes.

"I'd like to look over the parsonage house," said Jeph.

"No use. Old dame housekeeper has locked herself in, as savage as a bear with a sore head."

"Besides, they did turn over all the parson's things and made a bonfire of all his popish books. The little ones be dancing their rounds about it still!"

Stead had heard quite enough to make him very uneasy, and wish to get home with his tidings to his father. There was a girl standing by with a baby in her arms, and she asked:

"What will they do to our minister?"

"Put him in Little Ease for a scandalous minister," was the ready answer. "But he *is* a good man. He gave us all broth when father had the fever!"

"And who will give granny and me our Sunday dinner?" said a little boy.

"But there'll be no more catechising. Hurrah!" cried Oates, "hurrah!"

"'Tis rank superstition, said the red coat, Hurrah!" and up went their caps. "Halloa, Stead Kenton, not a word to say?"

"He likes being catechised, standing as he does like a stuck pig, and answering never a word," cried Jack.

"I do," said Steadfast, "and why not?"

"Parson's darling! Parson's darling!" shouted the boys. "A malignant! Off with him." They had begun to hustle him, when Jeph threw himself between and cried:

"Hit Steadfast, and you must hit me first."

"A match, a match!" they cried, "Jeph and Jack."

Stead had no fears about Jeph conquering, but while the others stood round to watch the boxing, he slipped away, with his heart perplexed and sad. He had loved his minister, and he never guessed how much he cared for his church till he saw it lying desolate, and these rude lads rejoicing in the havoc; while the words rang in his ears, "And now they break down all the carved work thereof with axes and with hammers."

CHAPTER IV

THE GOOD CAUSE

"And their Psalter mourneth with them
O'er the carvings and the grace,
Which axe and hammer ruin
In the fair and holy place."
Bp. CLEVELAND COXE.

When next John Kenton went into Bristol to market he tried to discover what had become of Mr. Holworth, but could only make out something about his being sent up to London with others of his sort to answer for being Baal worshippers! Which, as he observed, he could not understand.

There seemed likely to be no service at the church on Sunday, but John thought himself bound to walk thither with his sons to see what was going on, and they heard such a noise that they looked at each other in amazement. It was not preaching, but shouting, laughing, screaming, stamping, and running. The rude village children were playing at hide-and-seek, and Jenny Oates was hidden in the pulpit. But at Master Kenton's loud "How now, youngsters" they all were frightened, some ran out headlong, some sneaked out at the little north door, and the place was quiet, but in sad confusion and desolation, the altar-table overthrown, the glass of the windows lying in fragments on the pavement, the benches kicked over.

Kenton, with his boys' help, put what he could straight again, and then somewhat to their surprise knelt down with bowed head, and said a prayer, for they saw his lips moving. Then he locked up the church doors, for the keys had been left in them, and slowly and sadly went away.

"Thy mother would be sad to see this work," he said to Steadfast, as he stopped by her grave. "They say 'tis done for religion's sake, but I know not what to make of it."

The old Parish Clerk, North, had had a stroke the night after the plunder of the church, and lay a-dying and insensible. His wife gave his keys to Master Kenton, and on the following Sunday there was a hue-and-cry for them, and Oates the father, the cobbler, a meddling fellow, came down with a whole rabble of boys after him to the farm to demand them. "A preacher had come out from Bristol," he said, "a captain in the army, and he was calling for the keys to get into the church and give them a godly discourse. It would be the worse for Master Kenton if he did not give them up."

John had just sat down in the porch in his clean Sunday smock with the baby on his knee, and Rusha clinging about him waiting till Stead had cleaned himself up, and was ready to read to them from the mother's books.

When he understood Gates' message he slowly said, "I be in charge of the keys for this here parish."

"Come, come, Master Kenton, this wont do, give 'un up or you'll be made to. Times are changed, and we don't want no parsons nor churchwardens now, nor no such popery!"

"I'm accountable to the vestry for the church," gravely said Kenton. "I will come and see what is doing, and open the church if so be as the parish require it."

"Don't you see! The parish does—"

"I don't call you the parish, Master Gates, nor them boys neither," said Kenton, getting up however, and placing the little one in the cradle, as he called out to Patience to keep back the dinner till his return. The two boys and Rusha followed him to see what would happen.

Long before they reached the churchyard they heard the sound of a powerful voice, and presently they could see all the men and women of the parish as it seemed, gathered about the lych gate, where, on the large stone on which coffins were wont to be rested, stood a tall thin man, in a heavy broad-brimmed hat, large bands, crimson scarf, and buff coat, who was in fiery and eager words calling on all those around to awaken from the sleep of sloth and sin, break their bonds and fight for freedom and truth. He waved his long sword as he spoke and dared the armies of Satan to come on, and it was hard to tell which he really meant, the forces of sin, or the armies of men whom he believed to be fighting on the wrong side.

Someone told him that the keys of the church were brought, but he heeded not the interruption, except to thunder forth "What care I for your steeple house! The Church of God is in the souls of the faithful. Is it not written 'The kingdom of heaven is within you?' What, can ye not worship save between four walls?" And then he went on with the utmost fervour and vehemence, calling on all around to set themselves free from the chains that held them and to strive even to the death.

He meant all he said. He really believed he was teaching the only way of righteousness, and so his words had a force that went home to people's hearts as earnestness always does, and Jephthah, with tears in his eyes, began begging and praying his father to let him go and fight for the good Cause.

"Aye, aye," said Kenton, "against the world, the flesh, and the devil, and welcome, my son."

"Then I'll go and enlist under Captain Venn," cried Jeph.

"Not so fast, my lad. What I gave you leave for was to fight with the devil."

"You said the good Cause!"

"And can you tell me which be the good Cause?"

"Why, this here, of course. Did not you hear the Captain's good words, and see his long sword, and didn't they give five marks for Croppie's bull calf?"

"Fine words butter no parsnips," slowly responded Kenton.

"But," put in Steadfast, "butter is risen twopence the pound."

"Very like," said Kenton, "but how can that be the good Cause that strips the Churches and claps godly ministers into jail?"

Jephthah thought he had an answer, but fathers in those times did not permit themselves to be argued with.

Prices began going up still higher, for the Cavaliers were reported to be on their way to besiege Bristol, and the garrison wanted all the provisions they could lay in, and paid well for them. When Kenton and his boys went down to market, they found the old walls being strengthened with earth and stones, and sentries watching at the gates, but as they brought in provisions, and were by this time well known, no difficulty was made about admitting them.

One day, however, as they were returning, they saw a cloud of dust in the distance, and heard the sounds of drums and fifes playing a joyous tune. Kenton drew the old mare behind the bank of a high hedge, and the boys watched eagerly through the hawthorns.

Presently they saw the Royal Standard of England, though indeed that did not prove much, for both sides used it alike, but there were many lesser banners and pennons of lords and knights, waving on the breeze, and as the Kentons peeped down into the lane below they saw plumed hats, and shining corslets, and silken scarves, and handsome horses, whose jingling accoutrements chimed in with the tramp of their hoofs, and the notes of the music in front, while cheerful voices and laughter could be heard all around.

"Oh, father! these be gallant fellows," exclaimed Jephthah. "Will you let me go with these?"

Kenton laughed a little to himself. "Which is the good Cause, eh, son Jeph?"

He was, however, not at all easy about the state of things. "There is like to be fighting," he said to Steadfast, as they were busy together getting hay into the stable, "and that makes trouble even for quiet folks that only want to be let alone. Now, look you here," and he pulled out a canvas bag from the corner of the bin. "This has got pretty tolerably weighty of late, and I doubt me if this be the safest place for it."

Stead opened his eyes. The family all knew that the stable was used as the deposit for money, though none of the young folks had been allowed to know exactly where it was kept. There were no banks in those days, and careful people had no choice but either to hoard and hide, or to lend their money to someone in business.

The farmer poured out a heap of the money, all silver and copper, but he did not dare to wait to count it lest he should be interrupted. He tied up one handful, chiefly of pence, in the same bag, and put the rest into a bit of old sacking, saying, "You can get to the brook side, to the place you wot of, better than I can, Stead. Take you this with you and put it along with the other things, and then you will have something to fall back on in case of need. We'll put the rest back where it was before, for it may come handy."

So Steadfast, much gratified, as well he might be, at the confidence bestowed on him by his father, took the bag with him under his smock when he went out with the cows, and bestowed it in a cranny not far from that in which that more precious trust resided.

CHAPTER V

DESOLATION

"They shot him dead at the Nine Stonerig,
  Beside the headless Cross;
And they left him lying in his blood,
  Upon the moor and moss."
                              SURTEES.

More and more soldiers might be seen coming down the roads towards the town, not by any means always looking as gay as that first troop. Some of the feathers were as draggled as the old cock's tail after a thunderstorm, some reduced even to the quill, the coats looked threadbare, the scarves stained and frayed, the horses lean and bony.

There was no getting into the town now, and the growling thunder of a cannon might now and then be heard. Jeph would have liked to spend all his time on the hill-side where he could see the tents round the town, and watch bodies of troops come out, looking as small as toy soldiers, and see the clouds of smoke, sometimes the flashes, a moment or two before the report.

He longed to go down and see the camp, taking a load of butter and eggs, but the neighbours told his father that these troops were bad paymasters, and that there were idle fellows lurking about who might take his wares without so much as asking the price.

However, Jeph grew suddenly eager to herd the cattle, because thus he had the best chance of watching the long lines of soldiers drawn out from the camp, and seeing the smoke of the guns, whose sound made poor Patience stay and tremble at home, and hardly like to have her father out of her sight.

There was worse coming. Jeph had been warned to keep his cattle well out of sight from any of the roads, but when he could see the troops moving about he could not recollect anything else, and one afternoon Croppie strayed into the lane where the grass grew thick and rank, and the others followed her. Jeph had turned her back and was close to the farmstead when he heard shouts and the clattering of trappings. Half-a-dozen lean, hungry-looking troopers were clanking down the lane, and one called out, "Ha! good luck! Just what we want! Beef and forage. Turn about, young bumpkin, I say. Drive your cattle into camp. For the King's service."

"They are father's," sturdily replied Jeph, and called aloud for "Father."

He was answered with a rude shout of derision, and poor Croppie was pricked with the sword's point to turn her away. Jeph was wild with passion, and struck back the sword with his stick so unexpectedly that it flew out of the trooper's hand. Of course, more than one stout man instantly seized the boy, amid howls of rage; and one heavy blow had fallen on him, when Kenton dashed forward, thrusting himself between his son, and the uplifted arm, and had begun to speak, when, with the words "You will, you rebel dog?" a pistol shot was fired.

Jeph saw his father fall, but felt the grasp upon himself relax, and heard a voice shouting, "How now, my men, what's this?"

"He resisted the King's requisition, your Grace," said one of the troopers, as a handsome lad galloped up.

"King's requisition! Your own robbery. What have you done to the poor man, you Schelm? See here, Rupert," he added, as another young man rode hastily up.

"Rascals! How often am I to tell you that this is not to be made a place for your plunder and slaughter," thundered the new comer, rising in his stirrups, and striking at the troopers with the flat of his sword, so that they fell back with growls about "soldiers must live," and "curs of peasants."

The younger brother had leapt from his horse, and was trying to help Jephthah raise poor Kenton's head, but it fell back helplessly, deaf to the screams of "Father, father," with which Patience and Rusha had darted out, as a cloud of smoke began to rise from the straw yard. Poor children, they screamed again at what was before them. Rusha ran wildly away at sight of the soldiers, but Patience, with the baby in her arms, came up. She did not see her father at first, and only cried aloud to the gentlemen.

"O sir, don't let them do it. If they take our cows, the babe will die. He has no mother!"

"They shall not, the villains! Brother, can nothing be done?" cried the youth, with a face of grief and horror. And then there was a great confusion.

The two young officers were vehemently angry at sight of the fire, and shouted fierce orders to the guard of soldiers who had accompanied them to endeavour to extinguish it, themselves doing their best, and making the men release Steadfast, whom they had seized upon as he was trying to trample out the flame, kindled by a match from one of the soldiers who had scattered themselves about the yard during the struggle with Jephthah.

But either the fire was too strong, or the men did not exert themselves; it was soon plain that the house could not be saved, and the elder remounted, saying in German, "'Tis of no use, Maurice, we must not linger here."

"And can nothing be done?" again asked Prince Maurice. "This is as bad as in Germany itself."

"You are new to the trade, Maurice. You will see many such sights, I fear, ere we have done; though I hoped the English nature was more kindly."

Then using the word of command, sending his aides-de-camp, and with much shouting and calling, Prince Rupert got the troop together again, very sulky at being baulked of their plunder. They were all made to go out of the farm yard, and ride away before him, and then the two princes halted where the poor children, scarce knowing that their home was burning behind them, were gathered round their father, Patience stroking his face, Steadfast chafing his hands, Jephthah standing with folded arms, and a terrible look of grief and wrath on his face.

"Is there no hope?" asked Prince Maurice, sorrowfully.

"He is dead. That's all," muttered Jeph between his clenched teeth.

"Mark," said Prince Rupert, "this mischance is by no command of the King or mine. The fellow shall be brought to justice if you can swear to him."

"I would have hindered it, if I could," said the other prince, in much slower, and more imperfect English. "It grieves me much. My purse has little, but here it is."

He dropped it on the ground while setting spurs to his horse to follow his brother.

And thus the poor children were left at first in a sort of numb dismay after the shock, not even feeling that a heavy shower had begun to fall, till the baby, whom Patience had laid on the grass, set up a shriek.

Then she snatched him up, and burst into a bitter cry herself—wailing "father was dead, and he would die," in broken words. Steadfast then laid a hand on her, and said "He won't die, Patience, I see Croppie there, I'll get some milk. Take him."

There were only smoking walls, but the fire was burning down under the rain, and had not touched the stable, the wind being the other way. "Take him there," the boy said.

"But father—we can't leave him."

Without more words Jephthah and Steadfast took the still form between them and bore it into the stable, the baby screaming with hunger all the time, so that Jephthah hotly said—

"Stop that! I can't bear it."

Steadfast then said he would milk the cow if Jeph would run to the next cottage and get help. People would come when they knew the soldiers were gone.

There was nothing but Steadfast's leathern cap to hold the milk, and he felt as if his fingers had no strength to draw it; but when he had brought his sister enough to quiet little Ben, she recollected Rusha, and besought him to find her. She could hardly sit still and feed the little one while she heard his voice shouting in vain for the child, and all the time she was starting with the fancy that she saw her father move, or heard a rustling in the straw where her brothers had laid him.

And when little Ben was satisfied, she was almost rent asunder between her unwillingness to leave unwatched all that was left of her father, still with that vain hopeless hope that he might revive, all could not have been over in such a moment, and her terrible anxiety about her little sister. Could she have run back into the burning house? Or could those dreadful soldiers have killed her too?

Steadfast presently came back, having found some of the startled cattle and driven them in, but no Rusha. Patience was sure she could find her, and giving the baby to Steadfast ran out in the rain and smouldering smoke calling her; all in vain. Then she heard voices and feet, and in a fresh fright was about to turn again, when she knew Jephthah's call. He had the child in his arms. He had been coming back from the village with some neighbours, when they saw the poor little thing, crouched like a hare in her form under a bush. No sooner did she hear them, than like a hare, she started up to run away; but stumbling over the root of a tree, she fell and lay, too much frightened even to scream till her brother picked her up.

Kind motherly arms were about the poor girls. Old Goody Grace, who had been with them through their mother's illness, had hobbled up on hearing the terrible news. She looked like a witch, with a tall hat, short cloak, and nose and chin nearly meeting, but all Elmwood loved and trusted her, and the feeling of utter terror and helplessness almost vanished when she kissed and grieved over the orphans, and took the direction of things. She straightened and composed poor John Kenton's limbs, and gave what comfort she could by assuring the children that the passage must have been well nigh without pain. "And if ever there was a good man fit to be taken suddenly, it was he," she added. "He be in a happier place than this has been to him since your good mother was took."

Several of the men had accompanied her, and after some consultation, it was decided that the burial had better take place that very night, even though there was no time to make a coffin.

"Many an honest man will be in that same case," said Harry Blane, the smith, "if they come to blows down there."

"And He to Whom he is gone will not ask whether he lies in a coffin, or has the prayers said over him," added Goody, "though 'tis pity on him too, for he always was a man for churches and parsons and prayers."

"Vain husks, said the pious captain," put in Oates.

"Well," said Harry Blane, "those could hardly be vain husks that made John Kenton what he was. Would that the good old times were back again; when a sackless man could not be shot down at his own door for nothing at all."

Reverently and carefully John Kenton's body was borne to the churchyard, where he was laid in the grave beside his much loved wife. No knell was rung: Elmwood, lying far away over the hill side in the narrow wooded valley with the river between it and the camp, had not yet been visited by any of the Royalist army, but a midnight toll might have attracted the attention of some of the lawless stragglers. Nor did anyone feel capable of uttering a prayer aloud, and thus the only sound at that strange sad funeral was the low boom of a midnight gun fired in the beleaguered city.

Then Patience with Rusha and the baby were taken home by kind old Goody Grace, while the smith called the two lads into his house.

CHAPTER VI

LEFT TO THEMSELVES

"One look he cast upon the bier,
   Dashed from his eye the gathering tear,
   Then, like the high bred colt when freed
   First he essays his fire and speed,
   He vanished——"
                SCOTT.

Steadfast was worn and wearied out with grief and slept heavily, knowing at first that his brother was tossing about a good deal, but soon losing all perception, and not waking till on that summer morning the sun had made some progress in the sky.

Then he came to the sad recollection of the last dreadful day, and knew that he was lying on Master Blane's kitchen floor. He picked himself up, and at the same moment heard Jephthah calling him from the outside.

"Stead," he said, "I am going!"

"Going!" said poor Stead, half asleep.

"Yes. I shall never rest till I have had a shot at those barbarous German princes and the rest of the villains. My father's blood cries to me from the ground for vengeance."

"Would father have said like that?" said the boy, bewildered, but conscious of something defective, though these were Bible words.

"That's not the point! Captain Venn called every man to take the sword and hew down the wicked, and slay the ungodly and the murderers. I will!" cried Jeph, "none shall withhold me."

He had caught more phrases from these fiery preachers than he himself knew, and they broke forth in this time of excitement.

"But, Jeph, what is to become of us? The girls, and the little one! You are the only one of us who can do a man's work."

"I could not keep you together!" said Jeph. "Our house burnt by those accursed sons of Belial, all broken up, and only a lubber like you to help! No, Goody Grace or some one will take in the girls for what's left of the stock, and you can soon find a place—a strong fellow like you; Master Blane might take you and make a smith of you, if you be not too slow and clumsy."

"But Jeph—"

"Withhold me not. Is it not written—"

"I wish you would not say is it not written," broke in Stead, "I know it is, but you don't say it right."

"Because you are yet in darkness," said Jeph, contemptuously. "Hold your tongue. I must be off at once. Market folk can get into the town by the low lane out there, away from the camp of the spoilers, early in the morning, and I must hasten to enlist under Captain Venn. No, don't call the wenches, they would but strive to daunt my spirit in the holy work of vengeance on the bloodthirsty, and I can't abide tears and whining. See here, I found this in the corn bin. I'm poor father's heir. You won't want money, and I shall; so I shall take it, but I'll come back and make all your fortunes when I am a captain or a colonel. I wonder this is not more. We got a heap of late. Maybe father hid it somewhere else, but 'tis no use seeking now. If you light upon it you are welcome to do what you will with it. Fare thee well, Steadfast. Do the best you can for the wenches, but a call is laid on me! I have vowed to avenge the blood that was shed."

He strode off into the steep woodland path that clothed the hill side, and Steadfast looked after him, and felt more utterly deserted than before. Then he looked up to the sky, and tried to remember what was the promise to the fatherless children. That made him wonder whether the Bible and Prayer-book had been burnt, and then his morning's duty of providing milk for the little ones' breakfast pressed upon him. He took up a pail of Mrs. Blane's which he thought he might borrow and went off in search of the cows. So, murmuring the Lord's Prayer as he walked, and making the resolution not to be dragged away from his trust in the cavern, nor to forsake his little sister— he heard the lowing of the cows as he went over the hill, and found them standing at the gate of the fold yard, waiting to be eased of their milk. Poor creatures, they seemed so glad to welcome him that it was the first thing that brought tears to his eyes, and they came with such a rush that he had much ado to keep them from dropping into the pail as he leant his head against Croppie's ruddy side.

There was a little smouldering smoke; but the rain had checked the fire, and though the roof of the house was gone and it looked frightfully dreary and wretched, the walls were still standing and the pigs were grunting about the place. However, Steadfast did not stop to see what was left within, as he knew Ben would be crying for food, but he carried his foaming pail back to Goody Grace's as fast as he could, after turning out the cows on the common, not even stopping to count the sheep that were straggling about.

His sisters were watching anxiously from the door of Goody Grace's hovel, and eagerly cried out "Where's Jeph?"

Then he had to tell them that Jeph was gone for a soldier, to have his revenge for his father's death.

"Jeph gone too!" said poor Patience, looking pale. "Oh, what shall we ever do?"

"He did not think of that, I'll warrant, the selfish fellow," said Goody Grace. "That's the way with lads, nought but themselves."

"It was because of what they did to poor father," replied Stead.

"And if he, or the folks he is gone to, call that the Christian religion, 'tis more than I do!" rejoined the old woman. "I wish I had met him, I'd have given him a bit of my mind about going off to his revenge, as he calls it, without ever a thought what was to become of his own flesh and blood here."

"He did say I might go to service (not that I shall), and that some one would take you in for the cattle's sake."

"O don't do that, Stead," cried Patience, "don't let us part!" He had only just time to answer, "No such thing," for people were coming about them by this time, one after another emerging from the cottages that stood around the village green. The women were all hotly angry with Jeph for going off and leaving his young brothers and sisters to shift for themselves.

"He was ever an idle fellow," said one, "always running after the soldiers and only wanting an excuse."

"Best thing he could do for himself or them," growled old Green.

"Eh! What, Gaffer Green! To go off without a word or saying by your leave to his poor little sister before his good father be cold in his grave," exclaimed a whole clamour of voices.

"Belike he knew what a clack of women's tongues there would be, and would fain be out of it," replied the old man shrewdly.

It was a clamour that oppressed poor Patience and made her feel sick with sorrow and noise. Everybody meant to be very kind and pitiful, but there was a great deal too much of it, and they felt quite bewildered by the offers made them. Farmer Mill's wife, of Elmwood Cross, two miles off, was reported by her sister to want a stout girl to help her, but there was no chance of her taking Rusha or the baby as well as Patience. Goody Grace could not undertake the care of Ben unless she could have Patience, because she was so often called away from home, nor could she support them without the cows. Smith Blane might have taken Stead, but his wife would not hear of being troubled with Rusha. And Dame Oates might endure Rusha for the sake of a useful girl like Patience, but certainly not the baby. It was an utter Babel and confusion, and in the midst of it all, Patience crept up to her brother who stood all the time like a stock, and said "Oh! Stead, I cannot give up Ben to anyone. Cannot we all keep together?"

"Hush, Patty! That's what I mean to do, if you will stand by me," he whispered, "wait till all the clack is over."

And there he waited with Patience by his side while the parish seemed to be endlessly striving over them. If one woman seemed about to make a proposal, half-a-dozen more fell on her and vowed that the poor orphans would be starved and overworked; till she turned on the foremost with "And hadn't your poor prentice lad to go before the justices to shew the weals on his back?" "Aye, Joan Stubbs, and what are you speaking up for but to get the poor children's sheep? Hey, you now, Stead Kenton—Lack-a-day, where be they?"

For while the dispute was at its loudest and hottest, Stead had taken Rusha by the hand, made a sign to Patience, and the four deserted children had quietly gone away together into the copsewood that led to the little glen where the brook ran, and where was the cave that Steadfast looked on as his special charge. Rusha, frightened by the loud voices and angry gestures, had begun to cry, and beg she might not be given to anyone, but stay with her Patty and Stead.

"And so you shall, my pretty," said Steadfast, sitting down on the stump of a tree, and taking her on his knee, while Toby nuzzled up to them.

"Then you think we can go on keeping ourselves, and not letting them part us," said Patience, earnestly. "If I have done the house work all this time, and we have the fields, and all the beasts. We have only lost the house, and I could never bear to live there again," she added, with a shudder.

"No," said Steadfast, "it is too near the road while these savage fellows are about. Besides—" and there he checked himself and added, "I'll tell you, Patty. Do you remember the old stone cot down there in the wood?"

"Where the old hermit lived in the blind Popish times?"

"Aye. We'll live there. No soldiers will ever find us out there, Patty."

"Oh! oh! that is good," said Patience. "We shall like that, shan't we, Rusha?"

"And," added Steadfast, "there is an old cowshed against the rock down there, where we could harbour the beasts, for 'tis them that the soldiers are most after."

"Let us go down to it at once," cried the girl, joyfully.

But Steadfast thought it would be wiser to go first to the ruins of their home; before, as he said, anyone else did so, to see what could be saved therefrom.

Patience shrank from the spectacle, and Rusha hung upon her, saying the soldiers would be there, and beginning to cry. At that moment, however, Tom Gates' voice came near shouting for "Stead! Stead Kenton!"

"Come on, Stead. You'll be prentice-lad to Dick Stiggins the tailor, if so be you bring Whitefoot and the geese for your fee; and Goodman Bold will have the big wench; and Goody Grace will make shift with the little ones, provided she has the kine!"

"We don't mean to be beholden to none of them," said Steadfast, sturdily, with his hands in his pockets. "We mean to keep what belongs to us, and work for ourselves."

"And God will help us," Patience added softly.

"Ho, ho!" cried Tom, and proud of having found them, he ran before them back to the village green, and roared out, "Here they be! And they say as how they don't want none of you, but will keep themselves. Ha! ha!"

Anyone who saw those four young orphans would not have thought their trying to keep themselves a laughing matter; and the village folk, who had been just before so unwilling to undertake them, now began scolding and blaming them for their folly and ingratitude.

Nothing indeed makes people so angry as when a kindness which has cost them a great effort turns out not to be wanted.

"Look for nothing from us," cried Dame Bold. "I'd have made a good housewife of you, you ungrateful hussy, and now you may thank yourself, if you come to begging, I shall have nothing for you."

"Beggary and rags," repeated the tailor. "Aye, aye; 'tis all very fine strolling about after the sheep with your hands in your pockets in summer weather, but you'll sing another song in winter time, and be sorry you did not know when you had a good offer."

"The babe will die as sure as 'tis born," added Jean Oates.

"If they be not all slain by the mad Prince's troopers up in that place by the roadside," said another.

Blacksmith Blane and Goody Grace were in the meantime asking the children what they meant to do, and Stead told them in a few words. Goody Grace shook her head over little Ben, but Blane declared that after all it might be the best thing they could do to keep their land and beasts together. Ten to one that foolish lad Jephthah would come back with his tail between his legs, and though it would serve him right, what would they do if all were broken up? Then he slapped Stead on the back, called him a sensible, steady lad, and promised always to be his friend.

Moreover he gave up his morning's work to come with the children to their homestead, and see what could be saved. It was a real kindness, not only because his protection made Patience much less afraid to go near the place, and his strong arm would be a great help to them, but because he was parish constable and had authority to drive away the rough lads whom they found already hanging about the ruins, and who had frightened Patience's poor cat up into the ash tree.

The boys and two curs were dancing round the tree, and one boy was stripping off his smock to climb up and throw poor pussy down among them when Master Blane's angry shout and flourished staff put them all to flight, and Patience and Rusha began to coax the cat to come down to them.

Hunting her had had one good effect, it had occupied the boys and prevented them from carrying anything off. The stable was safe. What had been burnt was the hay rick, whence the flames had climbed to the house. The roof had fallen in, and the walls and chimney stood up blackened and dismal, but there was a good deal of stone about the house, the roof was of shingle, and the heavy fall, together with the pouring rain, had done much to choke the fire, so that when Blane began to throw aside the charred bits of beams and of the upper floor, more proved to be unburnt, or at least only singed, than could have been expected.

The great black iron pot still hung in the chimney with the very meal and kail broth that Patience had been boiling in it, and Rusha's little stool stood by the hearth. Then the great chest, or ark as Patience called it, where all the Sunday clothes were kept, had been crushed in and the upper things singed, but all below was safe. The beds and bedding were gone; but then the best bed had been only a box in the wall with an open side, and the others only chaff or straw stuffed into a sack.

Patience's crocks, trenchers, and cups were gone too, all except one horn mug; but two knives and some spoons were extracted from the ashes. Furniture was much more scanty everywhere than now. There was not much to lose, and of that they had lost less than they had feared.

"And see here, Stead," said Patience joyfully holding up a lesser box kept within the other.

It contained her mother's Bible and Prayer-book. The covers were turned up, a little warped by the heat, and some of the corners of the leaves were browned, but otherwise they were unhurt.

"I was in hopes 'twas the money box," said Blane.

"Jeph has got the bag," said Patience.

"More shame for him," growled their friend. Steadfast did not think it necessary to say that was not all the hoard.

Another thing about which Patience was very anxious was the meal chest. With much difficulty they reached it. It had been broken in by the fall of the roof, and some of the contents were scattered, but enough was gathered up in a pail fetched from the stable to last for some little time. There were some eggs likewise in the nests, and altogether Goodman Blane allowed that, if the young Kentons could take care of themselves, and keep things together, they had decided for the best; if they could, that was to say. And he helped them to carry their heavier things to the glen. He wanted to see if it were fit for their habitation, but Steadfast was almost sorry to show anyone the way, in spite of his trust and gratitude to the blacksmith.

However, of course, it was not possible to keep this strange hiding-place a secret, so he led the way by the path the cattle had trodden out through the brushwood to the open space where they drank, and where stood the hermit's hut, a dreary looking den built of big stones, and with rough slates covering it. There was a kind of hole for the doorway, and another for the smoke to get out at. Blane whistled with dismay at the sight of it, and told Stead he could not take the children to such a place.

"We will get it better," said Stead.

"That we will," returned Patience, who felt anything better than being separated from her brother.

"It is weather-tight," added Stead, "and when it is cleaned out you will see!"

"And the soldiers will never find it," added Patience.

"There is something in that," said Blane. "But at any rate, though it be summer, you can never sleep there to-night."

"The girls cannot," said Stead, "but I shall, to look after things."

These were long days, and by the evening many of the remnants of household stuff had been brought, the cows and Whitefoot had been tied up in their dilapidated shed, with all the hay Stead could gather together to make them feel at home. There was a hollow under the rock where he hoped to keep the pigs, but neither they nor the sheep could be brought in at present. They must take their chance, the sheep on the moor, the pigs grubbing about the ruins of the farmyard. The soldiers must be too busy for marauding, to judge by the constant firing that had gone on all day, the sharp rattle of the musquets, and now and then the grave roll of a cannon.

Stead had been too busy to attend, but half the village had been watching from the height, which accounted perhaps for the move from the farm having been so uninterrupted after the first.

It was not yet dark, when, tired out by his day's hard work, Stead sat himself down at the opening of his hut with Toby by his side. The evening gold of the sky could hardly be seen through the hazel and mountain-ash bushes that clothed the steep opposite bank of the glen and gave him a feeling of security. The brook rippled along below, plainly to be heard since all other sounds had ceased except the purring of a night-jar and the cows chewing their cud. There was a little green glade of short grass sloping down to the stream from the hut where the rabbits were at play, but on each side the trees and brushwood were thick, with only a small path through, much overgrown, and behind the rock rose like a wall, overhung with ivy and traveller's joy. Only one who knew the place could have found the shed among the thicket where the cows were fastened, far less the cavern half-way up the side of the rock where lay the treasures for which Steadfast was a watchman. He thought for a moment of seeing if all were safe, but then decided, like a wise boy, that to disturb the creepers, and wear a path to the place, was the worst thing he could do if he wished for concealment. He had had his supper at the village, and had no more to do, and after the long day of going to and fro, even Toby was too much tired to worry the rabbits, though he had had no heavy weights to carry. Perhaps, indeed, the poor dog had no spirits to interfere with their sports, as they sat upright, jumped over one another, and flashed their little white tails. He missed his old master, and knew perfectly well that his young master was in trouble and distress, as he crept close up to the boy's breast, and looked up in his face. Stead's hand patted the rough, wiry hair, and there was a sort of comfort in the creature's love. But how hard it was to believe that only yesterday he had a father and a home, and that now his elder brother was gone, and he had the great charge on him of being the mainstay of the three younger ones, as well as of protecting that treasure in the cavern which his father had so solemnly entrusted to him.

The boy knelt down to say his prayers, and as he did so, all alone in the darkening wood, the words "Father of the fatherless, Helper of the helpless," came to his aid.

CHAPTER VII

THE HERMIT'S GULLEY

"O Bessie Bell and Mary Grey,
   They were twa bonnie lasses—
They digged a bower on yonder brae,
   And theek'd it o'er wi' rashes."   BALLAD.

Steadfast slept soundly on the straw with Toby curled up by his side till the morning light was finding its way in through all the chinks of his rude little hovel.

When he had gathered his recollections he knew how much there was to be done. He sprang to his feet, showing himself still his good mother's own boy by kneeling down to his short prayer, then taking off the clothes in which he had slept, and giving himself a good bath in the pool under the bush of wax-berried guelder rose, and as good a wash as he could without soap.

Then he milked the cows, for happily his own buckets had been at the stable and thus were safe. He had just released Croppie and seen her begin her breakfast on the grass, when Patience in her little red hood came tripping through the glen with a broom over her shoulder, and without the other children. Goody Grace had undertaken to keep them for the day, whilst Patience worked with her brother, and had further lent her the broom till she could make another, for all the country brooms of that time were home-made with the heather and the birch. She had likewise brought a barley cake, on which and on the milk the pair made their breakfast, Goody providing for the little ones.

"We must use it up," said Patience, "for we have got no churn."

"And we could not get into the town to sell the butter if we had," returned her brother. "We had better take it up to some one in the village who might give us something for it, bread or cheese maybe."

"I would like to make my own butter," sighed Patience, whose mother's cleanly habits had made her famous for it.

"So you shall some day, Patty," said her brother, "but there's no getting into Bristol to buy one or to sell butter now. Hark! they are beginning again," as the growl of a heavy piece of cannon shook the ground.

"I wonder where our Jeph is," said the little girl sadly. "How could he like to go among all those cruel fighting men? You won't go, Stead?"

"No, indeed, I have got something else to do."

The children were hard at work all the time. They cleared out the inside of their hovel, which had a floor of what was called lime ash, trodden hard, and not much cracked. Probably other hermits in earlier times had made the place habitable before the expelled monk whom the Kentons' great-grandfather recollected; for the cell, though rude, was wonderfully strong, and the stone walls were very stout and thick, after the fashion of the middle ages. There was a large flat stone to serve as a hearth, and an opening at the top for smoke with a couple of big slaty stones bent towards one another over it as a break to the force of the rain. The children might have been worse off though there was no window, and no door to close the opening. That mattered the less in the summer weather, and before winter came, Stead thought he could close it with a mat made of the bulrushes that stood up in the brook, lifting their tall, black heads.

Straw must serve for their beds till they could get some sacking to stuff it into, and as some of the sheep would have to be killed and salted for the winter, the skins would serve for warmth. Patience arranged the bundles of straw with a neat bit of plaiting round them, at one corner of the room for herself and Rusha, at the opposite one for Stead. For the present they must sleep in their clothes.

Life was always so rough, and, to present notions, comfortless, that all this was not nearly so terrible to the farmer's daughter of two centuries ago as it would be to a girl of the present day. Indeed, save for the grief for the good father, the sense of which now and then rushed on them like a horrible, too true dream, Steadfast and Patience would almost have enjoyed the setting up for themselves and all their contrivances. Some losses, however, besides that of the churn were very great in their eyes. Patience's spinning wheel especially, and the tools, scythe, hook, and spade, all of which had been so much damaged, that Smith Blane had shaken his head over them as past mending.

Perhaps, however, Stead might borrow and get these made for him. As to the wheel, that must, like the churn, wait till the siege was over.

"But will not those dreadful men burn the town down and not leave one stone on another, if Jeph and the rest of them don't keep them out?" asked Patience.

"No," said Stead. "That is not the way in these days—at least not always. So poor father said last time we went into Bristol, when he had been talking to the butter-merchant's man. He said the townsfolk would know the reason why, if the soldiers were for holding out long enough to get them into trouble."

"Then perhaps there will not be much fighting and they will not hurt Jeph," said Patience, to whom Jeph was the whole war.

"There's no firing to-day. Maybe they are making it up," said Steadfast.

"I never heeded," said Patience, "we have been so busy! But Stead, how shall we get the things? We have no money. Shall we sell a sheep or a pig?"

Stead looked very knowing, and she exclaimed "Have you any, Stead? I thought Jeph took it all away."

Then Stead told her how his father had entrusted him with the bulk of the savings, in case of need, and had made it over to the use of the younger ones.

"It was well you did not know, Patty," he added. "You told no lie, and Jeph might have taken it all."

"O! he would not have been so cruel," cried Patience. "He would not want Rusha and Ben to have nothing."

Stead did not feel sure, and when Patience asked him where the hoard was, he shook his head, looked wise, and would not tell her. And then he warned her, with all his might and main against giving a hint to anyone that they had any such fund in reserve. She was a little vexed and hurt at first, but presently she promised.

"Indeed Stead, I won't say one word about it, and you don't think I would ever touch it without telling you."

"No, Patty, you wouldn't, but don't you see, if you know nothing, you can't tell if people ask you."

In truth, Stead was less anxious about the money than about the other treasure, and when presently Patience proposed that the cave where they used to play should serve for the poultry, so as to save them from the foxes and polecats, he looked very grave and said "No, no, Patty, don't you ever tell anyone of that hole, nor let Rusha see it."

"Oh! I know then!" cried Patience, with a little laugh, "I know what's there then."

"There's more than that, sister," and therewith Stead told in her ear of the precious deposit.

She looked very grave, and said "Why then it is just like church! O no, Stead, I'll never tell till good Mr. Holworth comes back. Could not we say our prayers there on Sundays?"

Stead liked the thought but shook his head.

"We must not wear a path up to the place," he said, "nor show the little ones the way."

"I shall say mine as near as I can," said Patience. "And I shall ask God to help us keep it safe."

Then the children became absorbed in seeking for a place where their fowls could find safe shelter from the enemies that lurked in the wood, and ended by an attempt of Stead's to put up some perches across the beam above the cow-shed.

Things were forward enough for Rusha and Ben to be fetched down to their new home that night; when Patience went to fetch them, she heard that the cessation of firing had really been because the troops within the town were going to surrender to the King's soldiers outside.

"Then there will be no more fighting," she anxiously asked of Master Blane.

"No man can tell," he answered.

"And will Jeph come back?"

But that he could tell as little, and indeed someone else spoke to him, and he paid the child no more attention.

Rusha had had a merry day among the children of her own age in the village; she fretted at coming away, and was frightened at turning into so lonely a path through the hazel stems, trotting after Patience because she was afraid to turn back alone, but making a low, peevish moan all the time.

Patience hoped she would be comforted when they came out on their little glade, and she saw Stead stirring the milk porridge over the fire he had lighted by the house. For he had found the flint and steel belonging to the matchlock of his father's old gun, and there was plenty of dry leaves and half-burnt wood to serve as tinder. The fire for cooking would be outside, whenever warmth and weather served, to prevent indoor smoke. And to Patience's eyes it really looked pleasant and comfortable, with Toby sitting wisely by his young master's side, and the cat comfortably perched at the door, and Whitefoot tied to a tree, and the cows in their new abode. But Jerusha was tired and cross, she said it was an ugly place, and she was afraid of the foxes and the polecats, she wanted to go home, she wanted to go back to Goody Grace.

Stead grew angry, and threatened that she should have no supper, and that made her cry the louder, and shake her frock at him; but Patience, who knew better how to deal with her, let her finish her cry, and come creeping back, promising to be good, and glad to eat the supper, which was wholesome enough, though very smoky: however, the children were used to smoke, and did not mind it.

They said their prayers together while the sun was touching the tops of the trees, crept into their hut, curled themselves up upon their straw and went to sleep, while Toby lay watchful at the door, and the cat prowled about in quest of a rabbit or some other evening wanderer for her supper.

The next day Patience spent in trying to get things into somewhat better order, and Steadfast in trying to gather together his live stock, which he had been forced to leave to take care of themselves. Horse, donkey, and cows were all safe round their hut; but he could find only three of the young pigs and the old sow at the farmyard, and it plainly was not safe to leave them there, though how to pen them up in their new quarters he did not know.

The sheep were out on the moor, and only one of them seemed to be missing. The goat and the geese had likewise taken care of themselves and seemed glad to see him. He drove them down to their new home, and fed them there with some of the injured meal. "But what can we do with the pigs? There's no place they can't get out of but this," said Stead, looking doubtfully.

"Do you think I would have pigs in here? No, I am not come to that!"

It ended in Stead's going to consult Master Blane, who advised that the younger pigs should be either sold, or killed and salted, and nothing left but the sow, who was a cunning old animal, and could pretty well take care of herself, besides that she was so tough and lean that one must be very hungry indeed to be greatly tempted by her bristles.

But how sell the pigs or buy the salt in such days as these? There was, indeed, no firing.

There was a belief that treaties were going on, but leisure only left the besiegers more free to go wandering about in search of plunder; and Stead found all trouble saved him as to disposing of his pigs. They were quite gone next time he looked for them, and the poor old sow had been lamed by a shot; but did not seem seriously hurt, and when with some difficulty she had been persuaded to be driven into the glen, she seemed likely to be willing to stay there in the corner of the cattle shed.

The children were glad enough to be in their glen, with all its bareness and discomfort, when they heard that a troop of horse had visited Elmwood, and made a requisition there for hay and straw. They had used no violence, but the farmers were compelled to take it into the camp in their own waggons, getting nothing in payment but orders on the treasury, which might as well be waste paper. And, indeed, they were told by the soldiers that they might be thankful to get off with their carts and horses.

CHAPTER VIII

STEAD IN POSSESSION

"At night returning, every labour sped,
He sits him down, the monarch of a shed."
GOLDSMITH.

Another day made it certain that the garrison of Bristol had surrendered to the besiegers. A few shots were heard, but they were only fired in rejoicing by the Royalists, and while Steadfast was studying his barley field, already silvered over by its long beards, and wondering how soon it would be ripe, and how he should get it cut and stacked, his name was shouted out, and he saw Tom Oates and all the rest of the boys scampering down the lane.

"Come along, Stead Kenton, come on and see, the Parliament soldiers come out and go by."

Poor Steadfast had not much heart for watching soldiers, but it struck him that he might see or hear something of Jephthah, so he came with the other boys to the bank, where from behind a hedge they could look down at the ranks of soldiers as they marched along, five abreast, the road was not wide enough to hold more. They had been allowed to keep their weapons, so the officers had their swords, and the men carried their musquets. Most of them looked dull and dispirited, and the officers had very gloomy, displeased faces. In fact, they were very angry with their commander, Colonel Fiennes, for having surrendered so easily, and he was afterwards brought to a court-martial for having done so.

Stead did not understand this, he thought only of looking under each steel cap or tall, slouching hat for Jephthah. Several times a youthful, slender figure raised his hopes, and disappointed him, and he began to wonder whether Jeph could have after all stayed behind in the town, or if he could have been hurt and was ill there.

By-and-by came a standard, bearing a Bible lying on a sword, and behind it rode a grave looking officer, with long hair, and a red scarf, whom the lads recognised as the same who had preached at Elmwood. His men were in better order than some of the others, and as Steadfast eagerly watched them, he was sure that he knew the turn of Jeph's head, in spite of his being in an entirely new suit of clothes, and with a musquet over his shoulder.

Stead shook the ash stem he was leaning against, the men looked up, he saw the well-known face, and called out "Jeph! Jeph!" But some of the others laughed, Jeph frowned and shook his head, and marched on. Stead was disappointed, but at any rate he could carry back the assurance to Patience that Jeph was alive and well, though he seemed to have lost all care for his brothers and sisters. Yet, perhaps, as a soldier he could not help it, and it might not be safe to straggle from the ranks.

There was no more fighting for the present in the neighbourhood. The princes and their army departed, only leaving a garrison to keep the city, and it was soon known in the village that the town was in its usual state, and that it was safe to go in to market as in former times. Stead accordingly carried in a basket of eggs, which was all he could yet sell. He was ferried across the river, and made his way in. It was strange to find the streets looking exactly as usual, and the citizens' wives coming out with their baskets just as if nothing had happened.

There was the good-natured face of Mistress Lightfoot, who kept a baker's shop at the sign of the Wheatsheaf, and was their regular customer.

"Ha, little Kenton, be'st thou there? I'm right glad to see thee. They said the mad fellows had burnt the farm and made an end of all of you, but I find 'em civil enow, and I'm happy to see 'twas all leasing-making."

"It is true, mistress," said Stead, "that they burnt our house and shot poor father."

"Eh, you don't say so, my poor lad?" and she hurried her kind questions, tears coming into her eyes, as she thought of the orphans deserted by their brother. She was very anxious to have Patience butter-making again and promised to come with Stead to give her assistance in choosing both a churn and a spinning wheel if he would come in the next day, for he had not ventured on bringing any money with him. She bought all his eggs for her lodger, good Doctor Eales, who could hardly taste anything and had been obliged to live cooped up in an inner chamber for fear of the Parliament soldiers, who were misbehaved to Church ministers though civil enough to women; while these new comers were just the other way, hat in hand to a clergyman, but apt to be saucy to the lasses. But she hoped the Doctor would cheer up again, now that the Cathedral was set in order, so far as might be, and prayers were said there as in old times. In fact the bells were ringing for morning prayer, and Stead was so glad to hear them that he thought he might venture in and join in the brief daily service. There were many others who had done so, for these anxious days had quickened the devotion of many hearts, and people had felt what it was to be robbed of their churches and forbidden the use of their prayer-books. Moreover, some had sons or brothers or husbands fighting on the one side or the other, and were glad to pray for them, so that Stead found himself in the midst of quite a congregation, though the choir had been too much dispersed and broken up for the musical service, and indeed the organ had been torn to pieces by the Puritan soldiers, who fancied it was Popish.

But Stead found himself caring for the Psalms and Prayers in a manner he had never done before, and which came of the sorrow he had felt and the troubles that pressed upon him. He fancied all would come right now, and that soon Mr. Holworth would be back, and he should be able to give up his charge; and he went home, quite cheered up.

When he came into the gulley he heard voices through the bushes, and pressing forward anxiously he saw Blane and Oates before the hovel door, Patience standing there crying, with the baby in her arms, and Rusha holding her apron, and an elderly man whom Stead knew as old Lady Elmwood's steward talking to the other men, who seemed to be persuading him to something.

As soon as Stead appeared, the other children ran up to him, and Rusha hid herself behind him, while Patience said "O Stead, Stead, he has come to turn us all out! Don't let him!"

"Nay, nay, little wench, not so fast," said the steward, not unkindly. "I am but come to look after my Lady's interests, seeing that we heard your poor father was dead, God have mercy on his soul (touching his hat reverently), and his son gone off to the wars, and nothing but a pack of children left."

"But 'tis all poor father's," muttered Stead, almost dumbfounded.

"It is held under the manor of Elmwood," explained the steward, "on the tenure of the delivery of the prime beast on the land on the demise of lord or tenant, and three days' service in hay and harvest time."

What this meant Steadfast and Patience knew as little as did Rusha or Ben, but Goodman Blane explained.

"The land here is all held under my Lady and Sir George, Stead—mine just the same—no rent paid, but if there's a death—landlord or tenant—one has to give the best beast as a fee, besides the work in harvest."

"And the question is," proceeded the steward, "who and what is there to look to. The eldest son is but a lad, if he were here, and this one is a mere child, and the house is burnt down, and here they be, crouching in a hovel, and how is it to be with the land. I'm bound to look after the land. I'm bound to look after my Lady's interest and Sir George's."

"Be they ready to build up the place if you had another tenant?" asked Blane, signing to Stead to hold his peace.

"Well—hum—ha! It might not come handy just now, seeing that Sir George is off with the King, and all the money and plate with him and most of the able-bodied servants, but I'm the more bound to look after his interests."

That seemed to be Master Brown's one sentence. But Blane took him up, "Look you here, Master Brown, I, that have been friend and gossip this many years with poor John Kenton—rest his soul—can tell you that your lady is like to be better served with this here Steadfast, boy though he be, than if you had the other stripling with his head full of drums and marches, guns and preachments, and what not, and who never had a good day's work in him without his father's eye over him. This little fellow has done half his share and his own to boot long ago. Now they are content to dwell down here, out of the way of the soldiering, and don't ask her ladyship to be at any cost for repairing the farm up there, but will do the best they can for themselves. So, I say, Master Brown, it will be a real good work of charity, without hurt to my Lady and Sir George to let them be, poor things, to fight it out as they can."

"Well, well, there's somewhat in what you say Goodman Blane, but I'm bound to look after my Lady's interests and Sir George's."

"I would come and work like a good one at my Lady's hay and harvest," said Stead, "and I shall get stronger and bigger every year."

"But the beast," said the steward, "my Lady's interests must come first, you see."

"O don't let him take Croppie," cried Patience. "O sir, not the cows, or baby will die, and we can't make the butter."

"You see, Master Brown," explained Blane, "it is butter as is their chief stand-by. Poor Dame Kenton, as was took last spring, was the best dairywoman in the parish, and this little maid takes after her. Their kine are their main prop, but there's the mare, there's not much good that she can do them."

"Let us look!" said the steward. "A sorry jade enow! But I don't know but she will serve our turn better than the cow. There was a requisition, as they have the impudence to call it, from the Parliament lot that took off all our horses, except old grey Dobbin and the colt, and this beast may come in handy to draw the wood. So I'll take her, and you may think yourself well off, and thank my Lady I'm so easy with you. 'Be not hard on the orphans,' she said. 'Heaven forbid, my Lady,' says I, 'but I must look after your interests.'"

The children hung round old Whitefoot, making much of her for the last time, and Patience and Rusha both cried sadly when she was led away; and it was hard to believe Master Blane, who told them it was best for Whitefoot as well as for themselves, since they would find it a hard matter to get food even for the more necessary animals in the winter, and the poor beast would soon be skin and bone; while for themselves the donkey could carry all they wanted to market; and it might be more important than they understood to be thus regularly accepted as tenants by the manor, so that no one could turn them out.

And Stead, remembering the cavern, knew that he ought to be thankful, while the two men went away, Brown observing, "One can scarce turn 'em out, poor things, but such a mere lubber as that boy is can do no good! If the elder one had thought fit to stay and mind his own business now!"

"A good riddance, I say," returned Blane. "Stead's a good-hearted lad, though clownish, and I'll do what I can for him."

CHAPTER IX

WINTRY TIMES

"Thrice welcome may such seasons be,
But welcome too the common way,
The lowly duties of the day."

There was of course much to do. Steadfast visited his hoard and took from thence enough to purchase churn, spinning wheel, and the few tools that he most needed; but it was not soon that Patience could sit down to spin. That must be for the winter, and their only chance of light was in making candles.

Rusha could gather the green rushes, though she could not peel them without breaking them; and Patience had to take them out of her hands and herself strip the white pith so that only one ribbon of green was left to support it.

The sheep, excepting a few old ewes, were always sold or killed before the winter, and by Blane's advice, Stead kept only three. The butcher Oates took some of the others, and helped Stead to dispose of four more in the market. Two were killed at different intervals for home use, but only a very small part was eaten fresh, as a wonderful Sunday treat, the rest was either disposed of among the neighbours, who took it in exchange for food of other kinds; or else was salted and dried for the winter's fare, laid up in bran in two great crocks which Stead had been forced to purchase, and which with planks from the half-burnt house laid over them served by turns as tables or seats. The fat was melted up in Patience's great kettle, and the rushes dipped in it over and over again till they had such a coating of grease as would enable them to be burnt in the old horn lantern which had fortunately been in the stable and escaped the fire.

Kind neighbours helped Stead to cut and stack his hay, and his little field of barley. All the grass he could cut on the banks he also saved for the animals' winter food, and a few turnips, but these were rare and uncommon articles only used by the most advanced farmers, and his father had only lately begun to grow them, nor had potatoes become known except in the gardens of the curious.

The vexation was that all the manor was called to give their three days' labour to Lady Elmwood's crops just as all their own were cut, and as, of course, Master Brown had chosen the finest weather, every one went in fear and trembling for their own, and Oates and others grumbled so bitterly at having to work without wage, that Blane asked if they called their own houses and land nothing.

There was fresh grumbling too that the food sent out to the labourers in the field was not as it used to be, good beef and mutton, but only bread and very hard cheese, and bowls of hasty pudding, with thin, sour small beer to wash it down. Oates growled and vowed he would never come again to be so scurvily used; and perhaps no one guessed that my lady was far more impoverished than her tenants, and had a hard matter to supply even such fare as this.

Happily the weather lasted good long enough to save the Kentons' little crop, though there was a sad remembrance of the old times, when the church bell gave the signal at sunrise for all the harvesters to come to church for the brief service, and then to start fair in their gleaning. The bell did still ring, but there were no prayers. The vicar had never come back, and it was reported that he had been sent to the plantations in America. There was no service on Sunday nearer than Bristol. It was the churchwardens' business to find a minister, and of these, poor Kenton was dead, and the other, Master Cliffe, was not likely to do anything that might put the parish to expense.

Goodman Blane, and some of the other more seriously minded folk used to walk into Bristol to church when the weather was tolerably fine. If it were wet, the little stream used to flood the lower valley so that it was not possible to get across. Steadfast was generally one of the party. Patience could not go, as it was too far for Rusha to walk, or for the baby to be carried.

Once, seeing how much she wished to go again to church, Stead undertook to mind the children, the cattle, and the dinner in her place; but what work he found it! When he tried to slice the onions for the broth, little Ben toddled off, and had to be caught lest he should tumble into the river. Then Rusha got hold of the knife, cut her hand, and rolled it up in her Sunday frock, and Steadfast, thinking he had got a small bit of rag, tied it up in Patience's round cap, but that he did not know till afterwards, only that baby had got out again, and after some search was found asleep cuddled up close to the old sow. And so it went on, till poor Steadfast felt as if he had never spent so long a day. As to reading his Bible and Prayer-book, it was quite impossible, and he never had so much respect for Patience before as when he found what she did every day without seeming to think anything of it.

She did not get home till after dark, but the Blanes had taken her to rest at the friends with whom they spent the time between services, and they had given her a good meal.

"Somehow," said Patience, "everybody seems kinder than they used to be before the fighting began—and the parsons said the prayers as if they had more heart in them."

Patience was quite right. These times of danger were making everyone draw nearer together, and look up more heartily to Him in Whom was there true help.

But winter was coming on and bringing bad times for the poor children in their narrow valley, so close to the water. It was not a very cold season, but it was almost worse, for it was very wet. The little brook swelled, turned muddy yellow, and came rushing and tumbling along, far outside its banks, so that Patience wondered whether there could be any danger of its coming up to their hut and perhaps drowning them.

"I think there is no fear," said Steadfast. "You see this house has been here from old times and never got washed away."

"It wouldn't wash away very easily," said Patience, "I wish we were in one of the holes up there."

"If it looks like danger we might get up," said Steadfast, and to please her he cleared a path to a freshly discovered cave a little lower down the stream, but so high up on the rocky sides of the ravine as to be safe from the water.

Once Patience, left at home watching the rushing of the stream, became so frightened that she actually took the children up there, and set Rusha to hold the baby while she dragged up some sheepskins and some food.

Steadfast coming home asked what she was about and laughed at her, showing her, by the marks on the trees, that the flood was already going down. Such alarms came seldom, but the constant damp was worse. Happily it was always possible to keep up a fire, wood and turf peat was plentiful and could be had for the cutting and carrying, and though the smoke made their eyes tingle, perhaps it hindered the damp from hurting them, when all the walls wept, in spite of the reed mats which they had woven and hung over them. And then it was so dark, Patience's rushes did not give light enough to see to do anything by them even when they did not get blown out, and when the sun had set there was nothing for it, but as soon as the few cattle had been foddered in their shed and cave, to draw the mat and sheepskins that made a curtain by way of door, fasten it down with a stone, share with dog and cat the supper of broth, or milk, or porridge which Patience had cooked, and then lie down on the beds of dried leaves stuffed into sacking, drawing over them the blankets and cloaks that had happily been saved in the chest, and nestling on either side of the fire, which, if well managed, would smoulder on for hours. There the two elder ones would teach Rusha her catechism and tell old stories, and croon over old rhymes till both the little ones were asleep, and then would hold counsel on their affairs, settle how to husband their small stock of money, consider how soon it would be expedient to finish their store of salted mutton and pork to keep them from being spoilt by damp, and wonder when their hens would begin to lay.

It could hardly be a merry Christmas for the poor children, though they did stick holly in every chink where it would go, but there were not many berries that year, and as Rusha said, "there were only thorns."

Steadfast walked to Bristol through slush and mire and rain, not even Smith Blane went with him, deeming the weather too bad, and thinking, perhaps, rather over much of the goose at home.

Bristol people were keeping Christmas with all their might, making the more noise and revelry because the Parliament had forbidden the feast to be observed at all. It was easy to tell who was for the King and who for the Parliament, for there were bushes of holly, mistletoe, and ivy, at all the Royalist doors and windows, and from many came the savoury steam of roast beef or goose, while the other houses were shut up as close as possible and looked sad and grim.

All the bells of all the churches were ringing, and everybody seemed to be trooping into them. As Steadfast was borne along by the throng, there was a pause, and a boy of his own age with a large hat and long feather, beneath which could be seen curls of jet-black hair, walked at the head of a party of gentlemen. Everyone in the crowd uncovered and there was a vehement outcry of "God save the King! God save the Prince of Wales!" Everyone thronged after him, and Steadfast had a hard struggle to squeeze into the Cathedral, and then had to stand all the time with his back against a pillar, for there was not even room to kneel down at first.

There was no organ, but the choir men and boys had rallied there, and led the Psalms which went up very loudly and heartily. Then the Dean went up into the pulpit and preached about peace and goodwill to men, and how all ought to do all in their power to bring those blessed gifts back again. A good many people dropped off during the sermon, and more after it, but Steadfast remained. He had never been able to come to the Communion feast since the evil times had begun, and he had thought much about it on his lonely walk, and knew that it was the way to be helped through the hard life he was living.

When all was over he felt very peaceful, but so hungry and tired with standing and kneeling so long after his walk, that he was glad to lean against the wall and take out the piece of bread that Patience had put in his wallet.

Presently a step came near, and from under a round velvet skull-cap a kind old face looked at him which he knew to be that of the Dean.

"Is that all your Christmas meal, my good boy?" he asked.

"I shall have something for supper, thank your reverence," replied Steadfast, taking off his leathern cap.

"Well, mayhap you could away with something more," said the Dean. "Come with me."

And as Steadfast obeyed, he asked farther, "What is your name, my child? I know your face in church, but not in town."

"No, sir, I do not live here. I am Steadfast Kenton, and I am from Elmwood, but we have no prayers nor sermon there since they took the parson away."

"Ah! good Master Holworth! Alas! my child, I fear you will scarce see him back again till the King be in London once more, which Heaven grant. And, meantime, Sir George Elmwood being patron, none can be intruded into his room. It is a sore case, and I fear me the case of many a parish besides."

Steadfast was so much moved by the good Dean's kindness as to begin to consider whether it would be betraying the trust to consult him about that strange treasure in the cave, but the lad was never quick of thought, and before he could decide one of the canons joined the Dean, and presently going up the steps to the great hall of the Deanery, Steadfast saw long tables spread with snowy napkins, trenchers laid all round, and benches on which a numerous throng were seating themselves, mostly old people and little children, looking very poor and ragged. Steadfast held himself to be a yeoman in a small way, and somewhat above a Christmas feast with the poor, but the Dean's kindness was enough to make him put away his pride, and then there was such a delicious steam coming up from the buttery hatch as was enough to melt away all nonsense of that sort from a hungry lad.

Grand joints of beef came up in clouds of vapour, and plum puddings smoked in their rear, to be eaten with them, after the fashion of these days, when of summer vegetables there were few, and of winter vegetables none. The choirmen and boys, indeed all the Cathedral clergy who were unmarried, were dining there too, but the Dean and his wife waited on the table where the poorest were. Horns of ale were served to everyone, and then came big mince pies. Steadfast felt a great longing to take his home to his sisters, but he was ashamed to do it, even though he saw that it was permissible, they were such beggarly-looking folks who set the example.

However, the Dean's wife came up to him with a pleasant smile and asked if he had no appetite or if he were thinking of someone at home, and when he answered, she kindly undertook to lend him a basket, for which he might call after evensong, and in the basket were also afterwards found some slices of the beef and a fine large cake.

Then the young Prince and his suite came in, and he stood at the end of the hall, smiling and looking amused as everyone's cup was filled with wine—such wine as the Roundhead captains had left, and the Dean at the head of the table gave out the health of his most sacred Majesty King Charles, might God bless him, and confound all his enemies! The Prince bared his black shining locks and drank, and there was a deep Amen, and then a hurrah enough to rend the old vaulted ceiling; and equally enthusiastically was the Prince's health afterwards drunk.

Stead heard the servants saying that such a meal had been a costly matter, but that the good Dean would have it so in order that one more true merry Christmas should be remembered in Bristol.

CHAPTER X

A TERRIBLE HARVEST DAY

"There is a reaper, whose name is death."
LONGFELLOW.

Spring came at last, cold indeed but dry, and it brought calves, and kids, and lambs, and little pigs, besides eggs and milk. The creatures prospered for two reasons no doubt. One was that Stead and Patience always prayed for a blessing on them, and the other was that they were almost as tender and careful over the dumb things as they were over little Ben, who could now run about and talk. All that year nothing particular happened to the children. Patience's good butter and fresh eggs had come to be known in Bristol, and besides, Stead and Rusha used to find plovers' eggs on the common, for which the merchants' ladies would pay them, or later for wild strawberries and for whortleberries. Stead could also make rush baskets and mats, and they were very glad of such earnings, some of which they spent on clothes, and on making their hut more comfortable, while some was stored up in case of need in the winter.

For another year things went on much in the same manner, Bristol was still kept by the King's troops; but when Steadfast went into the place there was less cheerfulness among the loyal folk, and the Puritans began to talk of victories of their cause, while in the Cathedral the canon's voice trembled and grew choked in the prayer for the King, and the sermons were generally about being true and faithful to King and church whatever might betide. The Prince of Wales had long since moved away, indeed there were reports that the plague was in some of the low, crowded streets near the water, and Patience begged her brother to take care of himself.

There had been no Christmas feast at the Deanery, it was understood that the Dean thought it better not to bring so many people together.

Then as harvest time was coming on more soldiers came into the place. They looked much shabbier than the troops of a year ago, their coats were worn and soiled, and their feathers almost stumps, but they made up for their poverty by swagger and noise, and Steadfast was thankful that it was unlikely that any of them should find the way to his little valley with what they called requisitions for the King's service, but which meant what he knew too well. Some of the villagers formed into bands, and agreed to meet at the sound of a cowhorn, to drive anyone off on either side, who came to plunder, and they even had a flag with the motto—

"If you take our cattle
We will give you battle."

And they really did drive off some stragglers. Stead, however, accepted the offer from Tom Gates of a young dog, considerably larger and stronger than poor old Toby, yellow and somewhat brindled, and known as Growler. He looked very terrible, but was very civil to those whom he knew, and very soon became devoted to all the family, especially to little Ben. However, most of the garrison and the poorer folk of the town were taken up with mending the weak places in the walls, and digging ditches with the earth of which they made steep banks, and there were sentries at the gates, who were not always civil. Whatever the country people brought into the town was eagerly bought up, and was paid for, not often in the coin of the realm, but by tokens made of tin or some such metal with odd stamps upon them, and though they could be used as money they would not go nearly so far as the sums they were held to represent—at least in anyone's hands but those of the officers.

There were reports that the Parliament army was about to besiege the town, and Prince Rupert was coming to defend it. Steadfast was very anxious, and would not let his sisters stir out of the valley, keeping the cattle there as much as possible.

One day, when he had been sent for to help to gather in Lady Elmwood's harvest, in the afternoon the reaping and binding were suddenly interrupted by the distant rattle of musketry, such as had been heard two years ago, in the time of the first siege but it was in quite another direction from the town. Everyone left off work, and made what speed they could to the top of the sloping field, whence they could see what was going on.

"There they be!" shouted Tom Gates. "I saw 'em first! Hurrah! They be at Luck's mill."

"Hush! you good-for-nothing," shrieked Bess Hart, throwing her apron over her head. "When we shall all be killed and murdered."

"Not just yet, dame," said Master Brown. "They be a long way off, and they have enow to do with one another. I wonder if Sir George be there. He writ to my lady that he hoped to see her ere long."

"And my Roger," called out a woman. "He went with Sir George."

"And our Jack," was the cry of another; while Steadfast thought of Jephthah, but knew he must be on the opposite side. From the top of the field, they could see a wide sweep of country dipping down less than two miles from them where there was a bridge over a small river, a mill, and one or two houses near. On the nearer side of the river could be seen the flash of steel caps, and a close, dark body of men, on the further side was another force, mostly of horsemen, with what seemed like waggons and baggage horses in the rear. They had what by its colours seemed to be the English banner, the others had several undistinguishable standards. Puffs of smoke broke from the windows of the mill.

"Aye!" said Goodman Blane. "I would not be in Miller Luck's shoes just now. I wonder where he is, poor rogue. Which side have got his mill, think you, Master Brown?"

"The round-headed rascals for certain," said Master Brown, "and the bridge too, trying to hinder the King's men from crossing bag and baggage to relieve the town."

"See, there's a party drawing together. Is it to force the bridge?"

"Aye, aye, and there's another troop galloping up stream. Be they running off, the cowards?"

"Not they. Depend on it some of our folks have told them of Colham ford. Heaven be with them, brave lads."

"Most like Sir George is there, I don't see 'em."

"No, of course not, stupid, they'll be taking Colham Lane. See, see, there's a lot of 'em drawn up to force the bridge. Good luck be with them."

More puffs of smoke from the mill, larger ones from the bank, and a rattle and roll came up to the watchers. There was a moment's shock and pause in the assault, then a rush forward, and the distant sound of a cheer, which those on the hill could not help repeating. But from the red coats on and behind the bridge, proceeded a perfect cloud of smoke, which hid everything, and when it began to clear away on the wind, there seemed to be a hand-to-hand struggle going on upon the bridge, smaller puffs, as though pistols were being used, and forms falling over the parapet, at which sight the men held their breath, and the women shrieked and cried "God have mercy on their poor souls." And then the dark-coated troops seemed to be driven back.

"That was a feint, only a feint," cried Master Brown. "See there!"

For the plumed troop of horsemen had indeed crossed, and came galloping down the bank with such a jingling and clattering, and thundering of hoofs as came up to the harvest men above, and Master Brown led the cheer as they charged upon the compact mass of red coats behind the bridge, and broke and rode them down by the vehemence of the shock.

"Hurrah!" cried Blane. "Surely they will turn now and take the fellows on the bridge in the rear. No. Ha! they are hunting them down on to their baggage! Well done, brave fellows, hip! hip!—"

But the hurrah died on his lips as a deep low hum—a Psalm tune sung by hundreds of manly voices—ascended to his ears, to the accompaniment of the heavy thud of horsehoofs, and from the London Road, between the bridge and the Royalist horsemen, there emerged a compact body of troopers, in steel caps and corslets. Forming in ranks of three abreast, they charged over the bridge, and speedily cleared off the Royalists who were struggling to obtain a footing there.

There was small speech on the hill side, as the encounter was watched, and the Ironsides forming on the other side, charged the already broken troops before they had time to rally, and there was nothing to be seen but an utter dispersion and scattering of men, looking from that distance like ants when their nest has been broken into.

It was only a skirmish, not to be heard of in history, but opening the way for the besiegers to the walls of Bristol, and preventing any of the supplies from reaching the garrison, or any of the intended reinforcements, except some of the eager Cavaliers, who galloped on thither, when they found it impossible to return and guard the bridge for their companions.

The struggle was over around the bridge in less than two hours, but no more of Lady Elmwood's harvest was gathered in that evening. The people watched as if they could not tear themselves from the contemplation of the successful bands gathering together in their solid masses, and marching onwards in the direction of Bristol, leaving, however, a strong guard at the bridge, over which piled waggons and beasts of burthen continued to pass, captured no doubt and prevented from relieving the city. It began to draw towards evening, and Master Brown was beginning to observe that he must go and report to my lady, poor soul; and as to the corn, well, they had lost a day gaping at the fight, and they must come up again to-morrow, he only hoped they were not carting it for the round-headed rogues; when at that moment there was a sudden cry, first of terror, then of recognition, "Roger, Hodge Fitter! how didst come here?"

For a weary, worn-out trooper, with stained buff coat, and heavy boots, stood panting among them. "I thought 'twas our folks," he said. "Be mother here?"

"Hodge! My Hodge! Be'st hurt, my lad?" cried the mother, bursting through the midst and throwing herself on him, while his father contented himself with a sort of grunt. "All right, Hodge. How com'st here?"

"And where's my Jack?" exclaimed Goody Bent.

"And where's our Harry?" was another cry from Widow Lakin.

While Stead longed to ask, but could not be heard in the clamour, whether his brother had been there.

Hodge could tell little—seen less than the lookers on above. He had been among those who had charged through the enemy, and ridden towards Bristol, but his horse had been struck by a stray shot, and killed under him. He had avoided the pursuers by scrambling through a hedge, and then had thought it best to make his way through the fields to his own home, until, seeing the party on the hill, he had joined them, expecting to find his parents among them.

Sir George he knew to be on before him, and probably almost at Bristol by this time. Poor Jack had been left weeks ago on the field of Naseby, though there had been no opportunity of letting his family know. "Ill news travels fast enough!" And as to Harry, he had been shot down by a trooper near about the bridge, but mayhap might be alive for all that.

"And my brother, Jeph Kenton," Steadfast managed to say. "Was he there?"

"Jeph Kenton! Why, he's a canting Roundhead. The only Elmwood man as is! More shame for him."

"But was he there?" demanded Stead.

"There! Well, Captain Venn's horse were there, and he was in them! I have seen him more than once on outpost duty, prating away as if he had a beard on his chin. I'd a good mind to put a bullet through him to stop his impudence, for a disgrace to the place."

"Then he was in the fight?" reiterated Steadfast.

"Aye, was he. And got his deserts, I'll be bound, for we went smack smooth through Venn's horse, like a knife through a mouldy cheese, and left 'em lying to the right and left. If the other fellows had but stuck by us as well, we'd have made a clean sweep of the canting dogs."

Hodge's eloquence was checked by the not unwelcome offer of a drink of cider.

"Seems quiet enough down there," said Nanny Lakin, peering wistfully over the valley where the shadows of evening were spreading. "Mayhap if I went down I might find out how it is with my poor lad."

"Nay, I'll go, mother," said a big, loutish youth, hitherto silent; "mayn't be so well for womenfolk down there."

"What's that to me, Joe, when my poor Harry may be lying a bleeding his dear life out down there?"

"There's no fear," said Hodge. "To give them their due, the Roundheads be always civil to country folk and women—leastways unless they take 'em for Irish—and thinking that, they did make bloody work with the poor ladies at

Naseby. But the dame there will be safe enough," he added, as she was already on the move down hill. "Has no one a keg of cider to give her? I know what 'tis to lie parching under a wound."

Someone produced one, and as her son shouted "Have with you, mother," Steadfast hastily asked Tom Oates to let Patience know that he was gone to see after Jephthah, and joined Ned Lakin and his mother.

Jeph had indeed left his brothers and sisters in a strange, wild way, almost cruel in its thoughtlessness; but to Stead it had never seemed more than that elder brotherly masterfulness that he took as a matter of course, and there was no resting in the thought of his lying wounded and helpless on the field— nay, the assurance that Hodge shouted out that the rebel dogs took care of their own fell on unhearing or unheeding ears, as Steadfast and Ned Lakin dragged the widow through a gap in the hedge over another field, and then made their way down a deep stony lane between high hedges.

It was getting dark, in spite of the harvest moon, by the time they came out on the open space below, and began to see that saddest of all sights, a battlefield at night.

A soldier used to war would perhaps have scorned to call this a battle, but it was dreadful enough to these three when they heard the sobbing panting, and saw the struggling of a poor horse not quite dead, and his rider a little way from him, a fine stout young man, cold and stiff, as Nanny turned up his face to see if it was her Harry's.

A little farther on lay another figure on his back, but as Nanny stooped over it, a lantern was flashed on her and a gruff voice called out, "Villains, ungodly churls, be you robbing the dead?" and a tall man stood darkly before them, pistol in hand.

"No, sir; no, sir," sobbed out Nanny. "I am only a poor widow woman, come down to see whether my poor lad be dead or alive and wanting his mother."

"What was his regiment?" demanded the soldier in a kinder voice.

"Oh, sir, your honour, don't be hard on him—he couldn't help it—he went with Sir George Elmwood."

"That makes no odds, woman, when a man's down," said the soldier. "Unless 'tis with the Fifth Monarchy sort, and I don't hold with them. I have an uncle and a cousin or two among the malignants, as good fellows as ever lived— no Amalekites and Canaanites—let Smite-them Derry say what he will. Elmwood! let's see—that was the troop that forded higher up, and came on Fisher's corps. This way, dame. If your son be down, you'll find him here; that is, unless he be carried into the mill or one of the houses. Most of the wounded lie there for the night, but the poor lads that are killed must be buried to-morrow. Take care, dame," as poor Nanny cried out in horror at having stumbled over a dead man's legs. He held his lantern so that she could see the face while she groaned out, "Poor soul." And thus they worked their sad way up to the buildings about the water mill. There was a shed through the chinks of which light could be seen, and at the door of which a soldier exclaimed—

"Have ye more wounded, Sam? There's no room for a dog in here. They lie as thick as herrings in a barrel."

"Nay, 'tis a poor country woman come to look for her son. What's his name? Is there a malignant here of the name of Harry Lakin?"

The question was repeated, and a cry of gladness, "Mother! mother!" ended in a shriek of pain in the distance within.

"Aye, get you in, mother, get you in. A woman here will be all the better, be she who she may."

The permission was not listened to. Nanny had already sprung into the midst of the mass of suffering towards the bloody straw where her son was lying.

Steadfast, who had of course looked most anxiously at each of the still forms on the way, now ventured to say:—

"So please you, sir, would you ask after one Jephthah Kenton? On your own side, sir, in Captain Venn's troop? I am his brother."

"Oh, ho! you are of the right sort, eh?" said the soldier. "Jephthah Kenton. D'ye know aught of him, Joe?"

"I heard him answer to the roll call before Venn's troop went off to quarters," replied the other man. "He is safe and sound, my lad, and Venn's own orderly."

Steadfast's heart bounded up. He longed still to know whether poor Harry Lakin was in very bad case, but it was impossible to get in to discover, and he was pushed out of the way by a party carrying in another wounded man, whose moans and cries were fearful to listen to. He thought it would be wisest to make the best of his way home to Patience, and set her likewise at rest, for who could tell what she might not have heard.

The moon was shining brightly enough to make his way plain, but the scene around was all the sadder and more ghastly in that pallid light, which showed out the dark forms of man and horse, and what was worse the white faces turned up, and those dark pools in which once or twice he had slipped as he saw or fancied he saw movements that made him shudder, while a poor dog on the other side of the stream howled piteously from time to time.

Presently, as he came near a hawthorn bush which cast a strangely shaped shadow, he heard a sobbing—not like the panting moan of a wounded man, but the worn out crying of a tired child. He thought some village little one must have wandered there, and been hemmed in by the fight, and he called out—

"Is anyone there?"

The sobbing ceased for a moment and he called again, "Who is it? I won't hurt you," for something white seemed to be squeezing closer into the bush.

"Who are you for?" piped out a weak little voice.

"I'm no soldier," said Steadfast. "Come out, I'll take you home by-and-by."

"I have no home!" was the answer. "I want father."

Steadfast was now under the tree, and could see that it was a little girl who was sheltering there of about the same size as Rusha. He tried to take her hand, but she backed against the tree, and he repeated "Come along, I wouldn't hurt you for the world. Who is your father? Where shall we find him?"

"My father is Serjeant Gaythorn of Sir Harry Blythedale's troopers," said the child, somewhat proudly, then starting again, "You are not a rebel, are you?"

"No, I am a country lad," said Steadfast; "I want to help you. Come, you can't stay here."

For the little hand she had yielded to him was cold and damp with the September dews. His touch seemed to give her confidence, and when he asked, "Can't I take you to your mother?" she answered—

"Mother's dead! The rascal Roundheads shot her over at Naseby."

"Poor child! poor child!" said Steadfast. "And you came on with your father."

"Yes, he took me on his horse over the water, and told me to wait by the bush till he came or sent for me, but he has not come, and the firing is over and it is dark, and I'm so hungry."

Steadfast thought the child had better come home with him, but she declared that father would come back for her. He felt convinced that her father, if alive, must be in Bristol, and that he could hardly come through the enemy's outposts, and he explained to her this view. To his surprise she understood in a moment, having evidently much more experience of military matters than he had, and when he further told her that Hodge was at Elmwood, and would no doubt rejoin his regiment at Bristol the next day, she seemed satisfied, and with the prospect of supper before her, trotted along, holding Steadfast's hand and munching a crust which he had found in his pouch, the remains of the interrupted meal, but though at first it seemed to revive her a good deal, the poor little thing was evidently tired out, and she soon began to drag, and fret, and moan. The three miles was a long way for her, and tired as he was, Steadfast had to take her on his back, and when at last he reached home, and would have set her down before his astonished sisters, she was fast asleep with her head on his shoulder.

CHAPTER XI

THE FORTUNES OF WAR

"Hear and improve, he pertly cries,
I come to make a nation wise."
                    GAY

Very early in the morning, before indeed anyone except Patience was stirring, Steadfast set forth in search of Roger Fitter to consult him about the poor child who was fast asleep beside Jerusha; and propose to him to take her into Bristol to find her father.

Hodge, who had celebrated his return by a hearty supper with his friends, was still asleep, and his mother was very unwilling to call him, or to think of his going back to the wars. However, he rolled down the cottage stair at last, and the first thing he did was to observe—

"Well, mother, how be you? I felt like a boy again, waking up in the old chamber. Where's my back and breast-piece? Have you a cup of ale, while I rub it up?"

"Now, Hodge, you be not going to put on that iron thing again, when you be come back safe and sound from those bloody wars?" entreated his mother.

"Ho, ho! mother, would you have me desert? No, no! I must to my colours again, or Sir George and my lady might make it too hot to hold you here. Hollo, young one, Stead Kenton, eh? Didst find thy brother? No, I'll be bound. The Roundhead rascals have all the luck."

"I found something else," said Steadfast, and he proceeded to tell about the child while Dame Fitter stood by with many a pitying "Dear heart!" and "Good lack!"

Hodge knew Serjeant Gaythorn, and knew that the poor man's wife had been shot dead in the flight from Naseby; but he demurred at the notion of encumbering himself with the child when he went into the town. He suspected that he should have much ado to get in himself, and if he could not find her father, what could he do with her?

Moreover, he much doubted whether the serjeant was alive. He had been among those on whom the sharpest attack had fallen, and not many of them had got off alive.

"What like was he?" said Steadfast. "We looked at a many of the poor corpses that lay there. They'll never be out of my eyes again at night!"

"A battlefield or two would cure that," grimly smiled Hodge. "Gaythorn—he was a man to know again—had big black moustaches, and had lost an eye, had a scar like a weal from a whip all down here from a sword-cut at Long Marston."

"Then I saw him," said Stead, in a low voice. "Did he wear a green scarf?"

"Aye, aye. Belonged to the Rangers, but they are pretty nigh all gone now."

"Under the rail of the miller's croft," added Stead.

"Just so. That was where I saw them make a stand and go down like skittles."

"Poor little maid. What shall I tell her?"

"Well, you can never be sure," said Hodge. "There was a man now I thought as dead as a door nail at Newbury that charged by my side only yesterday. You'd best tell the maid that if I find her father I'll send him after her; and if not, when the place is quiet, you might look at the mill and see if he is lying wounded there."

Steadfast thought the advice good, and it saved him from what he had no heart to do, though he could scarcely doubt that one of those ghastly faces had been the serjeant's.

When he approached his home he was surprised to hear, through the copsewood, the sound of chattering, and when he came in sight of the front of the hut, he beheld Patience making butter with the long handled churn, little Ben toddling about on the grass, and two little girls laughing and playing with all the poultry round them.

One, of course, was stout, ruddy, grey-eyed Rusha, in her tight round cap, and stout brown petticoat with the homespun apron over it; the other was like a fairy by her side; slight and tiny, dressed in something of mixed threads of white and crimson that shone in the sun, with a velvet bodice, a green ribbon over it, and a gem over the shoulder that flashed in the sun, a tiny scarlet hood from which such a quantity of dark locks streamed as to give something the effect of a goldfinch's crown, and the face was a brilliant little brown one, with glowing cheeks, pretty little white teeth, and splendid dark eyes.

Patience could have told that this bright array was so soiled, rumpled, ragged, and begrimed, that she hardly liked to touch it, but to Steadfast, who had only seen the child in the moonlight, she was a wonderful vision in the morning sunshine, and his heart was struck with a great pity at her clear, merry tones of laughter.

As he appeared in the open space, Toby running before him, the little girl looked up and rushed to him crying out—

"It's you. Be you the country fellow who took me home? Where's father?"

Stead was so sorry for her that he took her up in his arms and said—

"Hodge Fitter is gone into town to look for him, my pretty. You must wait here till he comes for you," and he would have kissed her, but she turned her head away, pouted, and said, "I didn't give you leave to do that, you lubber lad."

Steadfast was much diverted. He was now a tall sturdy youth of sixteen, in a short smock frock, long leathern gaiters, and a round straw hat of Patience's manufacture, and he felt too clumsy for the dainty little being, whom he hastened to set on her small feet—in once smart but very dilapidated shoes. His sisters were somewhat shocked at her impertinence and Rusha breathed out "Oh—!"

"I am to wait here for Serjeant Gaythorn," observed the little damsel somewhat consequentially. "Well! it is a strange little makeshift of a place, but 'tis the fortune of war, and I have been in worse."

"It is beautiful!" said Rusha, "now we have got a glass window—and a real door—and beds—" all which recent stages in improvement she enumerated with a gasp of triumph and admiration between each.

"So you think," said little Mistress Gaythorn. "But I have lived in a castle."

She was quite ready to tell her history. Her name was Emlyn, and the early part of the eight years of her life had been spent at Sir Harry Blythedale's castle, where her father had been butler and her mother my lady's woman. Sir Harry had gone away to the wars, and in his absence my lady had held out the castle (perhaps it was only a fortified house) against General Waller, hoping and hoping in vain for Lord Goring to come to her relief.

"That was worst of all," said Emlyn, "we had to hide in the cellars when they fired at us—and broke all the windows, and a shot killed my poor dear little kitten because she wouldn't stay down with me. And we couldn't get any water, except by going out at night; young Master George was wounded at the well. And they only gave us a tiny bit of dry bread and salt meat every day, and it made little Ralph sick and he died. And at last there was only enough for two days more—and a great breach—that's a hole," she added condescendingly,—"big enough to drive my lady's coach-and-six through in the court wall. So then my lady sent out Master Steward with one of the best napkins on the end of a stick—that was a flag of truce, you know—and all the rascal Roundheads had to come in, and we had to go out, with only just what we could carry. My lady went in her coach with Master George, because he was hurt, and the young ladies, and some of the maids went home; but the most of us kept with my lady, to guard her to go to his Honour and the King at Oxford. Father rode big Severn, and mother was on a pillion behind him, with baby in her arms, and I sat on a cushion in front."

After that, it seemed that my lady had found a refuge among her kindred, but that the butler had been enrolled in his master's troop of horse, and there being no separate means of support for his wife and children, they had followed the camp, a life that Emlyn had evidently enjoyed, although the baby died of the exposure. She had been a great pet and favourite with everybody, and no doubt well-cared for even after the sad day when her mother had perished in the slaughter at Naseby. Patience wondered what was to become of the poor child, if her father never appeared to claim her; but it was no time to bring this forward, for Steadfast, as soon as he had swallowed his porridge, had to go off to finish his day's labour for the lady of the manor, warning his sisters that they had better keep as close as they could in the wood, and not let the cattle stray out of their valley.

He had not gone far, however, before he met a party of his fellow labourers running home. Their trouble had been saved them. The Roundhead soldiers had taken possession of waggons, horses, corn and all, as the property of a malignant, and were carrying them off to their camp before the town.

Getting up on a hedge, Stead could see these strange harvestmen loading the waggons and driving them off. He also heard that Sir George had come late in the evening, and taken old Lady Elmwood and several of the servants into Bristol for greater safety. Then came the heavy boom of a great gun in the distance.

"The Parliament men are having their turn now—as the King's men had before," said Gates.

And all who had some leisure—or made it—went off to the church tower to get a better view of the white tents being set up outside the city walls, and the compact bodies of troops moving about as if impelled by machinery, while others more scattered bustled like insects about the camp.

Steadfast, however, went home, very anxious about his own three cows, and seven sheep with their lambs, as well as his small patches of corn, which, when green, had already only escaped being made forage of by the Royalist garrison, because he was a tenant of the loyal Elmwoods. These fields were exposed, though the narrow wooded ravine might protect the small homestead and the cattle.

He found his new guest very happy cracking nuts, and expounding to Rusha what kinds of firearms made the various sounds they heard. Patience had made an attempt to get her to exchange her soiled finery for a sober dress of Rusha's; but "What shall I do, Stead?" said the grave elder sister, "I cannot get her to listen to me, she says she is no prick-eared Puritan, but truly she is not fit to be seen." Stead whistled. "Besides that she might bring herself and all of us into danger with those gewgaws."

"That's true," said Stead. "Look you here, little maid—none can say whether some of the rebel folk may find their way here, and they don't like butterflies of your sort, you know. If you look a sober little brown bee like Rusha here, they will take no notice, but who knows what they might do it they found you in your bravery."

"Bravery," thought Patience, "filthy old rags, me seems," but she had the prudence not to speak, and Emlyn nodded her head, saying, "I'll do it for you, but not for her."

And when all was done, and she was transformed into a little russet-robed, white-capped being, nothing would serve her, but to collect all the brightest cranesbill flowers she could find, and stick them in her own bodice and Rusha's.

Patience could not at all understand the instinct for bright colours, but even little Ben shouted "Pretty, pretty."

Perhaps it was well that the delicate pink blossoms were soon faded and crushed, and that twilight veiled their colours, for just as the cattle were being foddered for the night, there was a gay step on the narrow path, and with a start of terror, Patience beheld a tall soldier, in tall hat, buff coat, and high boots before her; while Growler made a horrible noise, but Toby danced in a rapture of delight.

"Ha! little Patience, is't thou?"

"Jephthah," she cried, though the voice as well as the form were greatly changed in these two years between boyhood and manhood.

"Aye, Jephthah 'tis," he said, taking her hand, and letting her kiss him. "My spirit was moved to come and see how it was with you all, and to shew how Heaven had prospered me, so I asked leave of absence after roll-call, and could better be spared, as that faithful man, Hold-the-Faith Jenkins, will exhort the men this night. I came up by Elmwood to learn tidings of you. Ha, Stead! Thou art grown, my lad. May you be as much grown in grace."

"You are grown, too," said Patience, almost timidly. "What a man you are, Jeph! Here, Rusha, you mind Jeph, and here is little Benoni."

"You have reared that child, then," said Jeph, as the boy clung to his sister's skirts, "and you have kept things together, Stead, as I hardly deemed you would do, when I had the call to the higher service." It was an odd sort of call, but there was no need to go into that matter, and Stead answered gravely, "Yes, I thank God. He has been very good to us, and we have fared well.

Come in, Jeph, and see, and have something to eat! I am glad you are come home at last."

Jephthah graciously consented to enter the low hut. He had to bend his tall figure and take off his steeple-crowned hat before he could enter at the low doorway, and then they saw his closely cropped head.

Patience tarried a moment to ask Rusha what had become of Emlyn.

"She is hiding in the cow shed," was the answer. "She ran off as soon as she saw Jeph coming, and said he was a crop-eared villain."

This was not bad news, and they all entered the hut, where the fire was made up, and one of Patience's rush candles placed on the table with a kind of screen of plaited rushes to protect it from the worst of the draught. Jeph had grown quite into a man in the eyes of his brothers and sisters. He looked plump and well fed, and his clothes were good and fresh, and his armour bright, a contrast to Steadfast's smock, stained with weather and soil, and his rough leathern leggings, although Patience did her best, and his shirt was scrupulously clean every Sunday morning.

The soldier was evidently highly satisfied. "So, children, you have done better than I could have hoped. This hovel is weather-tight and quite fit to harbour you. You have done well to keep together, and it is well said that he who leaves all in the hands of a good Providence shall have his reward."

Jeph's words were even more sacred than these, and considerably overawed Patience, who, as he sat before her there in his buff coat and belt, laying down the law in pious language, was almost persuaded to believe that their present comfort and prosperity (such as it was) was owing to the faith which he said had led to his desertion of his family, though she had always thought it mere impatience of home work fired by revenge for his father's death.

No doubt he believed in this reward himself, in his relief at finding his brothers and sisters all together and not starving, and considered their condition a special blessing due to his own zeal, instead of to Steadfast's patient exertion.

He was much more disposed to talk of himself and the mercies he had received, but which the tone of his voice showed him to consider as truly his deserts. Captain Venn had, it seemed, always favoured him from the time of his enlistment and nothing but his youth prevented him from being a corporal. He had been in the two great battles of Marston Moor and Naseby, and come off unhurt from each, and moreover grace had been given him to interpret the Scriptures in a manner highly savoury and inspiriting to the soldiery.

Here Patience, in utter amaze, could not help crying out "Thou, Jeph! Thou couldst not read without spelling, and never would."

He waved his hand. "My sister, what has carnal learning to do with grace?" And taking a little black Bible from within his breastplate, he seemed about to give them a specimen, when Emlyn's impatience and hunger no doubt getting the better of her prudence, she crept into the room, and presently was seen standing by Steadfast's knee, holding out her hand for some of the bread and cheese on the table.

"And who is this little wench?" demanded Jeph, somewhat displeased that his brother manifested a certain inattention to his exhortation by signing to Patience to supply her wants. Stead made unusual haste to reply to prevent her from speaking.

"She is biding with us till she can join her father, or knows how it is with him."

"Humph! She hath not the look of one of the daughters of our people."

"Nay," said Steadfast. "I went down last night to the mill, Jeph, to see whether perchance you might be hurt and wanting help, and after I had heard that all was well with you, I lighted on this poor little maid crouching under a bush, and brought her home with me for pity's sake till I could find her friends."

"The child of a Midianitish woman!" exclaimed Jeph, "one of the Irish idolaters of whom it is written, 'Thou shalt smite them, and spare neither man, nor woman, infant, nor suckling.'" "But I am not Irish," broke out Emlyn, "I am from Worcestershire. My father is Serjeant Gaythorn, butler to Sir Harry Blythedale. Don't let him kill me," she cried in an access of terror, throwing herself on Steadfast's breast.

"No, no. He would not harm thee, on mine hearth. Fear not, little one, he *shall* not."

"Nay," said Jephthah, who, to do him justice, had respected the rights of hospitality enough not to touch his weapon even when he thought her Irish, "we harm not women and babes save when they are even as the Amalekites. Let my brother go, child. I touch thee not, though thou be of an ungodly seed; and I counsel thee, Steadfast, touch not the accursed thing, but rid thyself thereof, ere thou be defiled."

"I shall go so soon as father comes," exclaimed Emlyn. "I am sure I do not want to stay in this mean, smoky hovel a bit longer than I can help."

"Such are the thanks of the ungodly people," said Jeph, gravely rising. "I must be on my way back. We are digging trenches about this great city, assuredly believing that it shall be delivered into our hands."

"Stay, Jeph," said Patience. "Our corn! Will your folk come and cart it away as they have done my lady's?"

"The spoil of the wicked is delivered over to the righteous," said Jeph. "But seeing that the land is mine, a faithful servant of the good cause, they may not meddle therewith."

"How are they to know that?" said Steadfast, not stopping to dispute what rather startled him, since though Jeph was the eldest son, the land had been made over to himself. To save the crop was the point.

"Look you here," said Jeph, "walk down with me to my good Captain's quarters, and he will give you a protection which you may shew to any man who dares to touch aught that is ours, be it corn or swine, ox or ass."

It was a long walk, but Steadfast was only too glad to take it for the sake of such security, and besides, there was a real pleasure in being with Jeph, little as he seemed like the same idle, easy-going brother, except perhaps in those little touches of selfishness and boastfulness, which, though Stead did not realise them, did recall the original Jeph.

All through the moonlight walk Jeph expounded his singular mercies, which apparently meant his achievements in killing Cavaliers, and the commendations given to him. One of these mercies was the retention of the home and land, though he kindly explained that his brothers and sisters were welcome to get their livelihood there whilst he was serving with the army, but some day he should come home "as one that divideth the spoil," and build up the old house, unless, indeed, and he glanced towards the sloping woods of Elmwood Manor, "the house and fields of the malignants should be delivered to the faithful."

"My lady's house," said Steadfast under his breath.

"Wherefore not? Is it not written 'Goodly houses that ye builded not.' Thou must hear worthy Corporal Hold-the-Faith expound the matter, my brother."

They crossed the ferry and reached the outposts at last, and Stead was much startled when the barrel of a musquet gleamed in the moonlight, and a gruff voice said "Stand."

"The jawbone of an ass," promptly answered Jephthah.

"Pass, jawbone of an ass," responded the sentry, "and all's well. But who have you here, comrade!"

Jeph explained, and they passed up the narrow lane, meeting at the end of it another sentinel, with whom the like watchword was exchanged, and then they came out on a large village green, completely changed from its usual aspect by rows of tents, on which the moonlight shone, while Jeph seemed to know his way through them as well as if he were in the valley of Elmwood. Most of the men seemed to be asleep, for snores issued from sundry tents. In others there were low murmurings, perhaps of conversation, perhaps of prayer, for once Stead heard the hum of an "Amen." One or two men were about, and Jeph enquired of one if the Captain were still up, and heard that he was engaged in exercise with the godly Colonel Benbow.

Their quarters were in one of the best houses of the little village, where light gleamed from the window, and an orderly stood within the door, to whom Jeph spoke, and who replied that they were just in time. In fact two officers in broad hats and cloaks were just coming out, and Stead admired Jeph's military salute to them ere he entered the farmhouse kitchen, where two more gentlemen sat at the table with a rough plan of the town laid before them.

"Back again, Kenton," said his captain in a friendly tone. "Hast heard aught of thy brethren?"

"Yes, sir, I have found them well and in good heart, and have brought one with me."

"A helper in the good cause? Heaven be gracious to thee, my son. Thou art but young, yet strength is vouchsafed to the feeble hands."

"Please, sir," said Steadfast, who was twisting his hat about, "I've got to mind the others, and work for them."

"Yea, sir," put in Jeph, "there be three younger at home whom he cannot yet leave. I brought him, sir, to crave from you a protection for the corn and cattle that are in a sort mine own, being my father's eldest son. They are all the poor children have to live on."

"Thou shalt have it," said the captain, drawing his writing materials nearer to him. "There, my lad. It may be thou dost serve thy Maker as well by the plough as by the sword."

Steadfast pulled his forelock, thanked the captain, was reminded of the word for the night, and safely reached home again.

CHAPTER XII

FAREWELL TO THE CAVALIERS

"If no more our banners shew
Battles won and banners taken,
Still in death, defeat, and woe,
Ours be loyalty unshaken."
SCOTT

The next day the whole family turned out to gather in the corn. Rusha was making attempts at reaping, while Emlyn played with little Ben, who toddled about, shouting and chasing her in and out among the shocks. Now and again they paused at the low, thunderous growl of the great guns in the distance, in strange contrast to their peaceful work, and once a foraging party of troopers rode up to the gate of the little field, but Steadfast met them there, and showed the officer Captain Venn's paper.

"So you belong to Kenton of Venn's Valiants? It is well. A blessing on your work!" said the stern dark-faced officer, and on he went, happily not seeing Emlyn make an ugly face and clench her little fist behind him.

"How can you, Stead?" she cried. "I'd rather be cursed than blessed by such as he!"

Stead shook his head slowly. "A blessing is better than a curse any way," said he, but his mind was a good deal confused between the piety and good conduct of these Roundheads, in contrast with their utter contempt of the Church, and rude dealing with all he had been taught to hold sacred.

His harvest was, however, the matter in hand, and the little patch of corn was cut and bound between him and his sisters, without further interruption. The sounds of guns had ceased early in the day, and a neighbour who had ventured down to the camp to offer some apples for sale leant over the gate to wonder at the safety of the crop, "though to be sure the soldiers were very civil, if they would let alone preaching at you;" adding that there was like to be no more fighting, for one of the gentlemen inside had ridden out with a white flag, and it was said the Prince was talking of giving in.

"Give in!" cried Emlyn setting her teeth. "Never. The Prince will soon make an end of the rebels, and then I shall ride-a-cock horse with our regiment again! I shall laugh to see the canting rogues run!"

But the first thing Steadfast heard the next day was that the royal standard had come down from the Cathedral tower. He had gone up to Elmwood to get some provisions, and Tom Oates, who spent most of his time in gazing from the steeple, assured him that if he would come up, he would see for himself that the flags were changed. Indeed some of the foot soldiers who had been quartered in the village to guard the roads had brought the certain tidings that the city had surrendered and that the malignants, as they called the Royalists, were to march out that afternoon, by the same road as that by which the parliamentary army had gone out two years before.

This would be the only chance for Emlyn to rejoin her father or to learn his fate. The little thing was wild with excitement at the news. Disdainfully she tore off what she called Rusha's Puritan rags, though as that offended maiden answered "her own were *real* rags in spite of all the pains Patience had taken with them. Nothing would make them tidy," and Rusha pointed to a hopeless stain and to the frayed edges past mending.

"I hate tidiness. Only Puritan rebels are tidy!"

"We are not Puritans!" cried Rusha.

Emlyn laughed. "Hark at your names," she said. "And what's that great rebel rogue of a brother of yours?"

"Oh! he is Jeph! He ran away to the wars! But Stead isn't a Puritan," cried Rusha, growing more earnest. "He always goes to church—real church down in Bristol. And poor father was churchmartin, and knew all the parson's secrets."

"Hush, Rusha," said Patience, not much liking this disclosure, however Jerusha might have come by the knowledge, "you and Emlyn don't want to quarrel when she is just going to say good-bye!"

This touched the little girls. Rusha had been much enlivened by the little fairy who had seen so much of the world, and had much more playfulness than the hard-worked little woodland maid; and Emlyn, who in spite of her airs, knew that she had been kindly treated, was drawn towards a companion of her own age, was very fond of little Ben, and still more so of Steadfast.

Ben cried, "Em not go;" and Rusha held her hand and begged her not to forget.

"O no, I won't forget you," said Emlyn, "and when we come back with the King and Prince, and drive the Roundhead ragamuffins out of Bristol, then I'll bring Stead a protection for Croppie and Daisy and all, a silver bodkin for you, a Flanders lace collar for Patience, and a gold chain for Stead, and— But oh! wasn't that a trumpet? Stead! Stead! We must go, or we shall miss them." Then as she hugged and kissed them, "I'll tell Sir Harry and my lady how good you have been to me, and get my lady to make you a tirewoman, Rusha. And dear, dear little Ben shall be a king's guard all in gold."

Ben had her last smothering kiss, and Rusha began to cry and sob as the gay little figure, capering by Stead's side, disappeared between the stems of the trees making an attempt, which Steadfast instantly quenched, at singing,

"The king shall enjoy his own again."

Patience did not feel disposed to cry. She liked the child, and was grieved to think what an uncertain lot was before the merry little being, but her presence had made Rusha and Ben more troublesome than they had ever been in their lives before, and there was also the anxiety lest her unguarded tongue should offend Jeph and his friends.

Emlyn skipped along by Steadfast's side, making him magnificent promises. They paused by the ruins of the farm where Stead still kept up as much of the orchard and garden as he could with so little time and so far from home, and Emlyn filled her skirt with rosy-cheeked apples, saying in a pretty gentle manner, "they were such a treat to our poor rogues on a dusty march," and Stead aided her by carrying as many as he could.

However, an occasional bugle note, clouds of dust on the road far below in the valley, and a low, dull tramp warned them to come forward, and station themselves in the hedge above the deep lane where Steadfast had once watched for his brother. Only a few of the more adventurous village lads were before them now, and when Stead explained that the little wench wanted to watch for her father, they were kind in helping him to perch her in the hollow of a broken old pollard, where she could see, and not be seen. For the poor camp maiden knew the need of caution. She drew Steadfast close to her, and bade him not show himself till she told him, for some of the wilder sort would blaze away their pistols at anything, especially when they had had any good ale, or were out of sorts.

Poor fellows, there was no doubt of their being out of sorts, as they tramped along, half hidden in dust, even the officers, who rode before them, with ragged plumes and slouched hats. The silken banners, which they had been allowed to carry out, because of their prompt surrender, hung limp and soiled, almost like tokens of a defeat, and if any one of those spectators behind the hawthorns had been conversant with Roman history, it would have seemed to them like the passing under the yoke, so dejected, nay, ashamed was the demeanour of the gentlemen. Emlyn whispered name after name as they went by, but even she was hushed and overawed by the spectacle, as four abreast these sad remnants of the royal army marched along the lane, one or two trying to whistle, a few more talking in under tones, but all soon dying away, as if they were too much out of heart to keep anything up.

She scarcely stirred while the infantry, who were by far the most numerous, were going by, only naming corps or officer to Stead, then there came an interval, and the tread of horses and clank of their trappings could be heard. Then she almost forgot her precautions in her eagerness to crane forward. "They are coming!" she said. "All there are of them will be a guard for the Prince."

Stead felt a strange thrill of pain as he remembered the terrible scene when he had last beheld that tall, slight young figure, and dark face, now far sterner and sadder than in those early days, as Rupert went to meet the bitterest hour of his life.

Several gentlemen rode with him, whom Emlyn named as his staff, and then came more troopers, not alike in dress, being, in fact, remnants of shattered regiments. She was trembling all over with eagerness, standing up, and so leaning forward, that she might have tumbled into the lane, had not Steadfast held her.

At last came a scream. "There's Sir Harry! There's Dick! There's Staines! Oh! Dick, Dick, where's father?"

There was a halt, and bronzed faces looked up.

"Ha! Who's there?"

"I! I! Emlyn. Oh! Dick, is father coming?"

"Hollo, little one! Art thou safe after all?"

"I am, I am. Father! father! Come! Where is he?"

"It is poor Gaythorn's little wench," explained one of the soldiers, as Sir Harry, a grey-haired man, looking worn and weary, turned back, while Steadfast helped the child out on the bank with some difficulty, for her extreme haste had nearly brought her down, and she stood curtseying, holding out her arms, and quivering with hope that began to be fear.

"Poor child!" were the old gentleman's first words. "And where were you?"

"Please your honour, father left me in the thorn brake," said Emlyn, "and said he would come for me, but he did not; it got dark, and this country lad found me, and took me home. Is father coming, your honour?"

"Ah! my poor little maid, your father will never come again," said Sir Harry, sadly. "He went down by the mill stream. I saw him fall. What is to be done for her?" he added, turning to a younger gentleman, who rode by him, as the child stood as it were stunned for a moment. "This is the worst of it all. Heaven knows we freely sacrifice ourselves in the cause of Church and King, but it is hard to sacrifice others. Here are these faithful servants, their home broken up with ours, their children dying, and themselves killed—she, by the brutes after Naseby, he, in this last skirmish. 'Tis enough to break a man's heart. And what is to become of this poor little maid?"

"Oh! I'll go with your honour," cried Emlyn, stretching out her arms. "I can ride behind Dick, and I'll give no one any trouble. Oh! take me, sir."

"It cannot be done, my poor child," said Sir Harry. "We have no women with us now, and we have to make our way to Newark by forced marches to His Majesty. I have no choice but to bestow you somewhere till better times come. Hark you, my good lad, she says you found her, and have been good to her. Would your mother take charge of her? I'll leave what I can with you, and when matters are quiet, my wife, or the child's kindred, will send after her. Will your father and mother keep her for the present?"

"I have none," said Steadfast. "My father was killed in his own yard by some soldiers who wanted to drive our cows. Mother had died before, but my sister and I made a shift to take care of the little ones in a poor place of our own."

"And can you take the child in? You seem a good lad."

"We will do our best for her, sir."

"What's your name?" and "Where do you live?" followed. And as Steadfast replied the old Cavalier took out his tablets and noted them, adding, "Then you and your sister will be good to her till we can send after her."

"We will treat her like our little sister, sir."

"And here's something for her keep for the present, little enough I am afraid, but we poor Cavaliers have not much left. The King's men were well to do when I heard last of them, and they will make it up by-and-by. Or if not, my boy, can you do this for the love of God?"

"Yes, sir," said Steadfast, looking up with his honest eyes, and touching his forelock at the holy Name.

"Here, then," and Sir Harry held out two gold pieces, to which his companion added one, and two or three of the troopers, saying something about poor Gaythorn's little maid, added some small silver coins. There was something in Steadfast's mind that would have preferred declining all payment, but he was a little afraid of Patience's dismay at having another mouth to provide for all the winter, and he thought too that Jeph's anger at the adoption of the Canaanitish child might be averted if it were a matter of business and payment, so he accepted the sum, thanked Sir Harry and the rest, and renewed his promise to do the best in his power for the little maiden. He rather wondered that no questions were asked as to which side he held; but Sir Harry had no time to inquire, and could only hope that the honest, open face, respectful manner, clean dress, and the kindness which had rescued the child on the battlefield were tokens that he might be trusted to take care of the poor little orphan. Besides, many of the country people were too ignorant to understand the difference between the sides, but only took part with their squire, or if they loved their clergyman, clung to him. So the knight would not ask any questions, and only further called out "Fare thee well, then, poor little maid, we will send after thee when we can," and then giving a sharp, quick order, all the little party galloped off to overtake the rest.

Emlyn had been bred up in too much awe of Sir Harry to make objections, but as her friends rode off she gave a sharp shriek, screamed out one name after another, and finally threw herself down on the road bank in a wild passion of grief, anger, and despair, and when Steadfast would have lifted her up and comforted her, she kicked and fought him away. Presently he tried her again, begging her to come home.

"I won't! I won't go to your vile, tumble-down, roundhead, crop-eared hole!" she sobbed out.

"But, Sir Harry—"

"I won't! I say."

He was at his wits' end, but after all, the sound of other steps coming up startled her into composing herself and sitting up.

"Hollo, Stead Kenton! Got this little puppet on your hands?" said young Gates. "Hollo, mistress, you squeal like a whole litter of pigs."

"I am to take charge of her till her friends can send for her," said Stead, with protecting dignity.

"And that will be a long day! Ho, little wench, where didst get that sweet voice?"

"Hush, Tom! the child has only just heard that her father is dead."

This silenced the other lads, and Emlyn's desire to get away from them accomplished what Steadfast wished, she put her hand into his and let him lead her away, and as there were sounds of another troop of cavalry coming up the lane, the boys did not attempt to follow her. She made no more resistance, though she broke into fresh fits of moaning and crying all the way home, such as went to Steadfast's heart, though he could not find a word to comfort her.

Patience was scarcely delighted when Rusha darted in, crying out that Emlyn had come back again, but perhaps she was not surprised. She took the poor worn-out little thing in her arms, and rocked her, saying kind, tender little words, while Steadfast looked on, wondering at what girls could do, but not speaking till, finding that Emlyn was fast asleep, Patience laid her down on the bed without waking her, and then had time to listen to Stead's account of the interview with Sir Harry Blythedale.

"I could not help it, Patience," he said, "we couldn't leave the poor fatherless child out on the hedge-side."

"No," said Patience, "we can't but have her, as the gentleman said, for the love of God. He has taken care of us, so we ought to take care of the fatherless—like ourselves."

"That's right, Patience," said Steadfast, much relieved in his mind, "and see here!"

"I wonder you took that, Stead, and the poor gentlemen so ill off themselves."

"Well, Patience, I thought if you would not have her, Goody Grace might for the pay, but then who knows when any more may come?"

"Aye," said Patience, "we must keep her, though she will be a handful. Anyway, all this must be laid out for her, and the first chance I have, some shall be in decent clothes. I can't a-bear to see her in those dirty gewgaws."

CHAPTER XIII

GODLY VENN'S TROOP

"Ye abbeys and ye arches,
Ye old cathedrals dear,
The hearts that love you tremble,
And your enemies have cheer."
BP. CLEVELAND COXE.

"What would Jeph say?" was the thought of both Steadfast and Patience, as Emlyn ran about with Rusha and Ben, making herself tolerably happy and enlivening them all a good deal. After one fight she found that she must obey Patience, though she made no secret that she liked the sober young mistress of the hut much less than the others, and could even sometimes get Steadfast to think her hardly used, but he seldom showed that feeling, for he had plenty of sense, and could not bear to vex his sister; besides, he saw there would be no peace if her authority was not supported. It was a relief that there was no visit from Jeph for some little time, though the fighting was all over, and people were going in and out of Bristol as before.

Stead took the donkey with the panniers full of apples and nuts on market day, and a pile of fowls and ducks on its back, while he carried a basket of eggs on his arm, and in his head certain instructions from Patience about the grogram and linen he was to purchase for Emlyn, in the hope of making her respectable before Jeph's eyes should rest upon her. Stead's old customers were glad to see him again, especially Mrs. Lightfoot, who had Dr. Eales once again in her back rooms, keeping out of sight, while the good Dean was actually in prison for using the Prayer-book. Three soldiers were quartered upon her at the Wheatsheaf, and though, on the whole, they were more civil and much less riotous than some of her Cavalier lodgers had been, she was always in dread of their taking offence at the doctor and hauling him off to gaol.

Steadfast confided to her Patience's commission, which she undertook to execute herself. It included a spinning-wheel, for Patience was determined to teach Emlyn to spin, an art of which no respectable woman from the Queen downwards was ignorant in those days. As to finding his brother, the best way would be to ask the soldiers who were smoking in the kitchen where he was likely to be.

They said that the faithful and valiant Jephthah Kenton of Venn's horse would be found somewhere about the great steeple house, profanely called the Cathedral, for there the troops were quartered; and thither accordingly Stead betook himself, starting as he saw horses gearing or being groomed on the sward in the close which had always been kept in such perfect order. Having looked in vain outside for his brother, he advanced into the building, but he had only just had a view of horses stamping between the pillars, the floor littered down with straw, a fire burning in one of the niches, and soldiers lying about, smoking or eating, in all manner of easy, lounging attitudes, when suddenly there was a shout of "Prelatist, Idolater, Baal-worshipper, Papist," and to his horror he found it was all directed towards himself. They were pointing to his head, and two of them had caught him by the shoulders, when another voice rose "Ha! Let him alone. I say, Bill! Faithful! It's my brother. He knows no better!" Then dashing up, Jeph rammed the great hat down over Stead's brow, eyes and all, and called out, "Whoever touches my brother must have at me first."

"There," said one of the others, "the old Adam need not be so fierce in thee, brother Jephthah! No one wants to hurt the lad, young prelatist though he be, so he will make amends by burning their superstitious books on the fire, even as Jehu burnt the worshippers of Baal."

Steadfast felt somewhat as Christians of old may have felt when called on to throw incense on the altar of Jupiter, as a handful of pages torn from a Prayer-book was thrust into his hands. Words did not come readily to him, but he shook his head and stood still, perhaps stolid in resistance.

"Come," said Jeph, laying hold of his shoulder to drag him along.

"I cannot; 'tis Scripture," said Stead, as in his distress his eye fell on the leaves in his hand, and he read aloud to prove it—

"Thy Word is a lantern unto my feet, and a light unto my path."

There was one moment's pause. Perhaps the men had absolutely forgotten how much of their cherished Bible was integral in the hated Prayer-book; at any rate they were enough taken aback to enable Jeph to pull his brother out at the door, not without a fraternal cuff or two, as he exclaimed:

"Thou foolish fellow! ever running into danger for very dullness."

"What have I done, Jeph?" asked poor Stead, still bewildered.

"Done! Why, doffed thy hat, after the superstitious and idolatrous custom of our fathers."

"How can it be idolatrous? 'Twas God's house," said Stead.

"Aye, there thou art in the gall of bitterness. Know'st thou not that no house is more holy than another?" and Jeph would have gone on for some time longer, but that he heard sounds which made him suspect that someone had condemned the version of the Psalms as prelatical and profane, and that his comrades might yet burst forth to visit their wrath upon his young brother, whom he therefore proceeded to lead out of sight as fast as possible into the Dean's garden, where he had the entree as being orderly to Captain Venn, who, with other officers, abode in the Deanery.

There, controversy being dropped for the moment, Stead was able to tell his brother of his expedition, and how he had been obliged to keep the child, for very pity's sake, even if her late father's master had not begged him to do so, and given an earnest of the payment.

Jeph laughed a little scornfully at the notion of a wild Cavalier ever paying, but he was not barbarous, and allowed that there was no choice in the matter, as she could not be turned out to starve. When he heard that Stead had come with market produce he was displeased at it not having been brought up for the table of his officers, assuring Stead that they were not to be confounded with the roistering, penniless malignants, who robbed instead of paying. Stead said he always supplied Mistress Lightfoot, but this was laughed to scorn. "The rulers of the army of saints had a right to be served first, above all before one who was believed to harbour the idolater, even the priest of the groves."

Jeph directed that the next supply should come to the Deanery, as one who had the right of ownership, and Stead submitted, only with the secret resolve that Dr. Eales should not want his few eggs nor his pat of fresh butter.

Jeph was not unkind to Stead, and took him to dine with the other attendants of the officers in the very stone hall where he had eaten that Christmas dinner some twenty months before. There was a very long grace pronounced extempore, and the guests were stout, resolute, grave-looking men, who kept on their steeple-crowned hats all the time and conversed in low, deep voices, chiefly, as far as Stead could gather, on military matters, but they seemed to appreciate good beef and ale quite as much as any Cavalier trooper could have done. One of them noticing Stead asked whether he had come to take service with the saints and enjoy their dominion, but Jeph answered for him that his call lay at home among those of his own household, until his heart should be whole with the cause.

On the whole Stead was proud to see Jeph holding his own, though the youngest among these determined-looking men. These two years had made a man of the rough, idle, pleasure-loving boy, and a man after the Ironsides' fashion, grave, self-contained, and self-depending. Stead had been more like the elder than the younger brother in old times, but he felt Jeph immeasurably his elder in the new, unfamiliar atmosphere; and yet the boy had a strong sense that all was not right; that these were interlopers in the kind old Dean's house; that the talk about Baal was mere absurdity; and the profanation of the Cathedral would have been utterly shocking to his good father. His mind, however, worked slowly, and he would have had nothing to say even if he could have ventured to speak; but he was very anxious to get away; and when Jeph would have kept him to hear the serjeant expound a chapter of Revelation, he pleaded the necessity of getting home in time to milk the cows, and made his escape.

On the whole it was a relief that Jeph was too much occupied with his military duties to make visits to his home. It might not have been over easy to keep the peace between him and Emlyn, fiery little Royalist as she was, and too much used to being petted and fascinating everyone by her saucy audacity to be likely to be afraid of him.

If Patience crossed her she would have recourse to Stead, and he could seldom resist her coaxing, or be entirely disabused of the notion that his sister expected too much of her. And perhaps it was true. Patience was scarcely likely to understand differences of character and temperament, and not merely to recollect that Emlyn was only eighteen months younger than she had been when she had been forced into the position of the house mother. So, while Emlyn's wayward fancies were a great trial, Steadfast's sympathy with them was a greater one.

Stead continued to see Jeph when taking in the market produce, for which he was always duly paid. Jeph also wished the whole family to come in on Sunday to profit by the preaching of some of the great Independent lights; but Stead, after trying it once, felt so sure that Patience would be miserable at anything so unaccustomed, so thunderous, and, as it seemed to him, so abusive, that he held to it that the distance was too great, and that the cattle could not be left. The soldiery seemed to him to spend their spare time in defacing the many churches of the city, chiefly in order to do what they called purifying them from all idols, in which term they included every sort of carving or picture, or even figures on monuments.

And in this work of destruction a chest containing church plate had been come upon, making their work greedy instead of only mischievous.

When all the churches in Bristol had been ransacked, they began to extend their search to the parish churches in the neighbourhood, and Stead began to be very anxious, though he hoped and believed that the cave was a perfectly safe place.

CHAPTER XIV

THE QUESTION

"Dogged as does it."—TROLLOPE.

"Stead, Stead," cried Rusha, running up to him, as he was slowly digging over his stubble field to prepare it for the next crop, "the soldiers are in Elmwood."

"Yes," said Emlyn, coming up at the same time, "they are knocking about everything in the church and pulling up the floor."

"Patience sent us to get some salt," explained Rusha, "and we saw them from Dame Redman's door. She told us we had better be off and get home as fast as we could."

"But I thought we would come and tell you," added Emlyn, "and then you could get out the long gun and shoot them as they come into the valley— that is if you can take aim—but I would load and show you how, and then they would think it was a whole ambush of honest men."

"Aye, and kill us all—and serve us right," said Stead. "They don't want to hurt us if we don't meddle with them. But there's a good wench, Rusha, drive up the cows and sheep this way so that I can have an eye on them, and shew Captain Venn's paper, if any of those fellows should take a fancy to them."

"They are digging all over old parson's garden," said Rusha, as she obeyed.

"Was Jeph there?" asked Stead.

"I didn't see him," said the child.

Steadfast was very uneasy. That turning up the parson's garden looked as if they might be in search of the silver belonging to the Church, but after all they were unlikely to connect him with it, and it was wiser to go on with his regular work, and manifest no interest in the matter; besides that, every spadeful he heaved up, every chop he gave the stubble, seemed to be a comfort, while there was a prayer on his soul all the time that he might be true to his trust.

By-and-by he saw Tom Oates running and beckoning to him, "Stead, Stead Kenton, you are to come."

"What should I come for?" said Stead, gruffly.

"The soldiers want you."

"What call have they to me?"

"They be come to cleanse the steeple house, they says, and take the spoil thereof, and they've been routling over the floor and parson's garden like so many hogs, and are mad because they can't find nothing, and Thatcher Jerry says, says he, 'Poor John Kenton as was shot was churchwarden and was very great with Parson. If anybody knows where the things is 'tis Steadfast Kenton.' So the corporal says, 'Is this so, Jephthah Kenton?' and Jeph, standing up in his big boots, says, 'Aye, corporal, my father was yet in the darkness of prelacy, and was what in their blindness they call a Churchwarden, but as to my brother, that's neither here nor there, he were but a boy and not like to know more than I did.' But the corporal said, 'That we will see. Is the lad here?' So I ups and said nay, but I'd seen you digging your croft, and then they bade me fetch you. So you must come, willy-nilly, or they may send worse after you."

Stead was a little consoled by hearing that his brother was there. He suspected that Jeph would have consideration enough for his sisters and for the property that he considered his own to be unwilling to show the way to their valley; and he also reflected that it would be well that whatever might happen to himself should be out of sight of his sisters. Therefore he decided on following Oates, going through on the way the whole question whether to deny all knowledge, and yet feeling that the things belonging to God should not be shielded by untruth. His resolution finally was to be silent, and let them make what they would out of that, and Stead, though it was long since he had put it on, had a certain sullen air of stupidity such as often belongs to such natures as his, and which Jeph knew full well in him.

They came in sight of the village green where the soldiers were refreshing themselves at what once had been the Elmwood Arms, for though not given to excess, total abstinence formed no part of the discipline of the Puritans; and one of the men started forward, and seizing hold of Steadfast by the shoulder exclaimed—

"As I live, 'tis the young prelatist who bowed himself down in the house of Rimmon! Come on, thou seed of darkness, and answer for thyself."

If he had only known it, he was making the part of dogged silence and resistance infinitely easier to Steadfast by the rudeness and abuse, which, even in a better cause, would have made it natural to him to act as he was doing now, giving the soldier all the trouble of dragging him onward and then standing with his hands in his pockets like an image of obstinacy.

"Speak," said the corporal, "and it shall be the better for thee. Hast thou any knowledge where the priests of Baal have bestowed the vessels of their mockery of worship."

Stead moved not a muscle of his face. He had no acquaintance with priests of Baal or their vessels, so that he was not in the least bound to comprehend, and one of them exclaimed "The oaf knows not your meaning, corporal. Speak plainer to his Somerset ears. He knows not the tongue of the saints."

"Ho, then, thou child of darkness. Know'st thou where the mass-mongering silver and gold of this church be hidden from them of whom it is written 'haste to the spoil.' Come, speak out. A crown if thou dost speak—the lash if thou wilt not answer, thou dumb dog."

Stead was really not far removed from a dumb dog. All his faculties were so entirely wrought up to resistance that he had hardly distinguished the words.

"Come, come, Stead," said Jeph, "thou art too old for thine old sulky moods. Speak up, and tell if thou know'st aught of the Communion Cup and dish, or it will be the worse for thee. Yes or no?"

Stead made a move with his shoulder to push away his brother, and still stood silent.

"There," said Jeph, "it is all Faithful's fault for his rough handling. His back is set up. It was always so from a boy, and you'll get nought out of him."

"Foolishness is bound in the heart of a child, but the rod of correction shall drive it far from him," quoted the Corporal, taking up a waggoner's whip which stood by the inn door, and the like of which had no doubt once been a more familiar weapon to him than the sword.

"Speak lad—or—" and as no speech came, the lash descended on Stead's shoulders, not, however, hurting him much save where it grazed the skin of his face.

"Now? Not a word? Take off his leathern coat, Faithful, then shall he feel the reward of sullenness."

That Jeph did not interfere, while Faithful and another soldier tugged off his leathern coat, buffeting and kicking him roughly as they did so, brought additional hardness to Stead. He had been flogged in his time before, and not without reason, and had taken a pride in not giving in, or crying out for pain; and the ancient habit acquired in a worse cause, came to his help. He scarcely recollected the cause of his resistance; all his powers were concentrated in holding out, and when after another "Now, vile prelatic spawn, is thy heart still hardened? Yes or no?" the terrible whip came stinging and biting down on his shoulders and back, only protected by his shirt, he was entirely bound up in the determination to endure the pain without a groan or cry.

But after blows enough had fallen to mark the shirt with streaks of blood, Jeph could bear it no longer.

"Hold!" he said. "You will never make him speak that way. Father and mother never could. Strokes do but harden him."

"The sure token of a fool," said the corporal, and prepared for another lash.

"'Tis plain he knows," said one of the others. "He would never stand this if a word would save him."

"Mere malice and obstinacy," said Faithful, "and wilfulness. He will not utter a word. I would beat it out of him, as I was wont with our old ass."

Another stroke descended, worse than all the others after the brief interval, but Jeph again spoke, "Look you, I know the lad of old and you'll get no more that way than if you were flogging the sign-post there. Whether he knows where the things are or not, the temper that is in him will never answer while you beat him, were it to save his life. Leave him to me, and I'll be bound to get an answer from him."

"And I am constable, and I must say," said Blacksmith Blane, moving forwards, with a bar of iron in his hand, and four or five stout men behind him, "that to come and abuse and flog a hard-working, fatherless lad, that never did you no harm, nor anyone else, is not what honest men look for from soldiers that talk so big about Parliament and rights and what not!"

"'Twas for contumacy," began the corporal.

"Contumacy forsooth, as though 'twas the will of the honest gentlemen in Parliament that boys should be misused for nothing at all!"

"If the young dog would have spoken," began the corporal, but somehow he did not like the look of Blane's iron bar, and thought it best to look up at the sun, and discover that it was time to depart if the party were to be in time for roll-call. As it was a private marauding speculation, it might not be well to have complaints made to Captain Venn, who never sanctioned plunder nor unnecessary violence. Even Jeph had to march off, and Steadfast, who had no mind to be pitied, nor asked by the neighbours what was the real fact, had picked up his spade and jerkin, and was out of sight while the villagers were watching the soldiers away.

The first thing he did was to give thanks in heart that he had been aided thus far not to betray his trust, and then to feel that Corporal Dodd's flogging was a far severer matter than the worst chastisement he had ever received from his father, even when he kept Jeph's secret about the stolen apples. Putting on his coat was impossible, and he was so stiff and sore that he could not hope to conceal his condition from Patience.

At home all were watching for him. They ran up in anxiety, for one of the ever ready messengers of evil had rushed down the glen to tell Patience that the soldiers were beating Stead shamefully, and Jeph standing by not saying one word. Little Ben broke out with "Poor, poor!" and Rusha burst into tears at sight of the blood, while Emlyn said "Just what comes of going among the rascal Roundheads," and Patience looked up at him and said "Was it—?" he nodded, and she quietly said "I'm glad." He added, "Jeph's coming soon," and she knew that the trial was not over. The brother and sister needed very few words to understand one another, and they were afraid to say anything that the younger ones could understand. Patience washed the weals with warm water and milk, and wrapped a cloak round him, but even the next morning, he could not use his arms without fresh bleeding, and the hindrance to the work was serious. He could do nothing but herd the cattle, and he was much inclined to drive them to the further end of the moorland where Jephthah would hardly find him, but then he recollected that Patience would be left to bear the brunt of the attack, so that he would not go far off, never guessing, poor fellow, that in his dull, almost blundering fashion, he was doing like the heroes and the martyrs, but only feeling that he must keep his trust at all costs. Jeph, however, did not come that day or the next, so that inwardly, the wound-up feeling had passed into a weariness of expectation, and outwardly the stripes had healed enough for Stead to go about his work as usual only a little stiffly. He went into Bristol on market day as usual, and then it was, on his way out that Jeph joined him, saying it was to bid Patience and the little ones farewell, since the marching orders were for the morrow. He was unusually kind and good-natured; he had a load of comfits for Rusha and Ben, and a stout piece of woollen stuff for Patience which he said was such as he was told godly maidens wore, and which possibly the terror of his steel cap and corslet had cheapened at the mercer's; also he had a large packet of tractates for Stead's own reading, and he enquired whether they possessed a Bible.

Stead wondered whether all this was out of regret at the treatment he had undergone, or whether it was to put him off his guard, and this occupied him when Jeph began to preach, as he did uninterruptedly for the last mile, without any of the sense, if there were any, reaching the mind of the auditor.

They reached the hut, the gifts were displayed; and when the young ones, who were all a little afraid of the elder brother, had gone off to feast upon the sweets, Jeph began with enquiries after Steadfast's back, and he replied that it was mending fast, while Patience exclaimed at the cruelty and wickedness of so using him.

"Why wouldn't he speak then?" said Jeph. "Yea or nay would have ended it in a moment, but that's Stead's way. He looks like it now!" and he did, elbows on knees, and chin on hands.

"Come now, Stead, thou canst speak to me! Was it all because Faithful hauled thee about?"

"He did, and he had no call to," said Stead, surlily.

"Well, that's true, but I'm not hauling thee. Tell me, Stead, I mind now that thou wast out with father that last day ere the Parson was taken to receive his deserts. I don't believe that even thy churlishness would have stood such blows if thou hadst known naught of the idolatrous vessels, and couldst have saved thy skin by saying so! No answer. Why, what have these malignants done for thee that thou shouldst hold by them? Slain thy father! Burnt thine house! No fault of theirs that thou art alive this day! Canst not speak?"

Jeph's temper giving way at the provocation, he forgot his conciliatory intentions and seizing Stead by the collar shook him violently. Growler almost broke his chain with rage, Patience screamed and flew to the rescue, just as she had often done when they were all children together, and Jeph threw his brother from him so that he fell on the root of a tree, and lay for a moment or two still, then picked himself up again evidently with pain, though he answered Patience cheerfully that it was nought.

"Thou art enough to drive a man mad with thy surly silence," exclaimed Jeph, whom this tussle had rendered much more like his old self, "and after all, knowing that even though thou art not one of the holy ones, thou wilt not tell a lie, it comes to the same thing. I know thou wottest where these things are, and it is only thy sullen scruples that hinder thee from speaking. Nevertheless, I shall leave no stone unturned till I find them! For what is written 'Thou shalt break down their altars.'"

"Jeph," said Stead, firmly. "You left home because of your grief and rage at father's death. Would you have me break the solemn charge he laid on me?"

"Father was a good man after his light," said Jeph, a little staggered, "but that light was but darkness, and we to whom the day itself is vouchsafed are not bound by a charge laid on us in ignorance. Any way, he laid no bonds on me, but I must needs leave thee alone in thy foolishness of bondage! Come, Patience, wench, and aid me, I know this rock is honeycombed with caves, like a rabbit warren, no place so likely."

"I help thee—no indeed'" cried Patience. "Would I aid thee to do what would most grieve poor father, that thou once mad'st such a work about! I should be afraid of his curse."

Possibly if Jeph had not pledged himself to his comrades to overcome his brother's resistance, and bring back the treasures, he might have desisted; but what he did was to call to Rusha to bring him a lantern, and show him the holes, promising her a tester if she would. She brought the lantern, but she was a timid, little, unenterprising thing, and was mortally afraid of the caverns, a fear that Patience had thought it well not to combat. Emlyn who had already scrambled all over the face of the slope, and peeped into all, could have told him a great deal more about them; but she hated the sight of a rebel, and sat on the ground making ugly faces and throwing little stones after him whenever his back was turned.

Stead, afraid to betray by his looks of anxiety, when Jeph came near the spot, sat all the time with his elbows on his knees, and his hands over his face, fully trusting to what all had agreed at the time of the burial of the chest, that there was no sign to indicate its whereabouts.

He felt rather than saw that Jeph, after tumbling out the straw and fern that served for fodder in the lower caves, where the sheep and pigs were sheltered in winter, had scrambled up to the hermit's chapel, when suddenly there was a shout, but not at all of exultation, and down among the bushes, lantern and all came the soldier, tumbling and crashing into the midst of an enormous bramble, whence Stead pulled him out with the lantern flattened under him, and his first breathless words were—

"Beelzebub himself!" Then adding, as he stood upright, "he made full at me, and I saw his eyes glaring. I heard him groaning. It is an unholy popish place. No wonder!"

Patience and Rusha were considerably impressed, for it was astonishing to see how horribly terrified and shaken was the warrior, who had been in two pitched battles, and Ben screamed, and needed to be held in Stead's arms to console him.

Jeph had no mind to pursue his researches any further. He only tarried long enough to let Patience pick out half-a-dozen thorns from his cheeks and hands, and to declare that if he had not to march to-morrow, he should bring that singular Christian man, Captain Venn, to exorcise the haunt of Apollyon. Wherewith he bade them all farewell, with hopes that by the time he saw them again, they would have come to the knowledge of the truth.

No sooner was he out of sight among the bushes than Emlyn seized on Rusha, and whirled her round in a dance as well as her more substantial proportions would permit, while Steadfast let his countenance expand into the broad grin that he had all this time been stifling.

"What *do* you think it was?" asked Patience, still awestruck.

"Why—the old owl—and his own bad conscience. He might talk big, but he didn't half like going against poor father. Thank God! He has saved His own, and that's over!"

CHAPTER XV

A TABLE OF LOVE IN THE WILDERNESS

"Yet along the Church's sky
Stars are scattered, pure and high;
Yet her wasted gardens bear
Autumn violets, sweet and rare,
Relics of a Spring-time clear,
Earnests of a bright New Year."   KEBLE

No more was heard or seen of Jephthah, or of Captain Venn's troop. The garrison within Bristol was small and unenterprising, and in point of fact the war was over. News travelled slowly, but Stead picked up scraps at Bristol, by which he understood that things looked very bad for the King. Moreover, Sir George Elmwood died of his wounds; poor old Lady Elmwood did not long survive him, and the estate, which had been left to her for her life, was sequestrated by the Parliament, and redeemed by the next heir after Sir George, so that there was an exchange of the Lord of the Manor. The new squire was an elderly man, hearty and good-natured, who did not seem at all disposed to interfere with any one on the estate. He was a Presbyterian, and was shocked to find that the church had been unused for three years. He had it cleaned from the accumulation of dirt and rubbish, the broken windows mended with plain glass, and the altar table put down in the nave, as it had been before Mr. Holworth's time; and he presented to the living Mr. Woodley, a scholarly-looking person, who wore a black gown and collar and bands.

The Elmwood folk were pleased to have prayers and sermon again, and Patience was glad that the children should not grow up like heathens; but her first church going did not satisfy her entirely.

"It is all strange," she said to Stead, who had stayed with the cattle. "He had no book, and it was all out of his own head, not a bit like old times."

"Of course not," said Emlyn. "He had got no surplice, and I knew him for a prick-eared Roundhead! I should have run off home if you had not held me, Patience. I'll never go there again."

"I am sure you made it a misery to me, trying to make Rusha and Ben as idle and restless as yourself," said Patience.

"They ought not to listen to a mere Roundhead sectary," said Emlyn, tossing her head. "I couldn't have borne it if I had not had the young ladies to look at. They had got silk hoods and curls and lace collars, so as it was a shame a mere Puritan should wear."

"O Emlyn, Emlyn, it is all for the outside," said Patience. "Now, I did somehow like to hear good words, though they were not like the old ones."

"Good, indeed! from a trumpery Puritan."

Stead went to church in the afternoon. He was eighteen now, and that great struggle and effort had made him more of a man. He thought much when he was working alone in the fields, and he had spent his time on Sundays in reading his Bible and Prayer-book, and comparing them with Jeph's tracts. Since Emlyn had come, he had made a corner of the cowshed fit to sleep in, by stuffing the walls with dry heather, and the sweet breath of the cows kept it sufficiently warm, and on the winter evenings, he took a lantern there with one of Patience's rush lights, learnt a text or two anew, and then repeated passages to himself and thought over them. What would seem intolerably dull to a lad now, was rest to one who had been rendered older than his age by sorrow and responsibility, and the events that were passing led people to consider religious questions a great deal.

But Stead was puzzled. The minister was not like the soldiers whom he had heard raving about the reign of the saints, and abusing the church. He prayed for the King's having a good deliverance from his troubles, and for the peace of the kingdom, and he gave out that there was to be a week of fasting, preaching, and preparation for the Sacrament of the Lord's Supper.

The better sort of people in the village were very much pleased, nobody except Goody Grace was dissatisfied, and people told her that was only because she was old and given to grumbling at everything new. Blane the Smith tapped Stead on the shoulder, and said, "Hark ye, my lad. If it be true that thou wast in old Parson's secrets, now's the time for thou know'st what."

Stead's mouth was open, and his face blank, chiefly because he did not know what to do, and was taken by surprise, and Blane took it for an answer.

"Oh! if you don't know, that's another thing, but then 'twas for nothing that the troopers flogged you? Well," he muttered, as Stead walked off, "that's a queer conditioned lad, to let himself be flogged, as I wouldn't whip a dog, all out of temper, because he wouldn't answer a question. But he's a good lad, and I'll not bring him into trouble by a word to squire or minister."

The children went off to gather cowslips, and Stead was able to talk it over with Patience, who at first was eager to be rid of the dangerous trust, and added, with a sigh, "That she had never taken the Sacrament since the Easter before poor father was killed, and it must be nigh upon Whitsuntide now."

"That's true," said Stead, "but nobody makes any count of holy days now. It don't seem right, Patience."

"Not like what it used to be," said Patience. "And yet this minister is surely a godly man."

"Father and parson didn't say ought about a godly man. They made me take my solemn promise that I'd only give the things to a lawfully ordained minister."

"He is a minister, and he comes by law," argued Patience. "Do be satisfied, Stead. I'm always in fear now that folks guess we have somewhat in charge; and Emlyn is such a child for prying and chattering. And if they should come and beat thee again, or do worse. Oh, Stead! surely you might give them up to a good man like that; Smith Blane says you ought!"

"I doubt me! I know that sort don't hold with Bishops, and, so far as I can see, by father's old Prayer-book, a lawful minister must have a Bishop to lay hands on him," said Stead, who had studied the subject as far as his means would allow, and had good though slow brains of his own, matured by responsibility. "I'll tell you what, Patience, I'll go and see Dr. Eales about it. I wot he is a minister of the old sort, that father would say I might trust to."

Dr. Eales was still living in Mrs. Lightfoot's lodgings, at the sign of the Wheatsheaf, or more properly starving, for he had only ten pounds a year paid to him out of the benefice that had been taken away from him; and though that went farther then than it would do now, it would not have maintained him, but that his good hostess charged him as little as she could afford, and he also had a few pupils among the gentry's sons, but there were too many clergymen in the same straits for this to be a very profitable undertaking. There were no soldiers in Mrs. Lightfoot's house now, and the doctor lived more at large, but still cautiously, for in the opposite house, named the "Ark," whose gable end nearly met the Wheatsheaf's, dwelt a rival baker, a Brownist, whose great object seemed to be to spy upon the clergyman, and have something to report against him, nor was Mrs. Lightfoot's own man to be trusted. Stead lingered about the open stall where the bread was sold till no customer was at hand, and then mentioned under his breath to the good dame his desire to speak with her lodger.

"Certainly," she said, but the Doctor was now with his pupils at Mistress Rivett's. He always left them at eleven of the clock, more shame of Mrs. Rivett not to give the good man his dinner, which she would never feel. Steadfast had better watch for him at the gate which opened on the down, for there he could speak more privately and securely than at home.

He took the advice, and passed away the time as best he could, learning on the way that a news letter had been received stating that the King was with the Scottish army at Newcastle, and that it was expected that on receiving their arrears of pay, the Scots would surrender him to the Parliament, a proceeding which the folk in the market-place approved or disapproved according to their politics.

Mrs. Rivett's house stood a little apart from the town, with a court and gates opening on the road over the down; and just as eleven strokes were chiming from the town clock below, a somewhat bent, silver-haired man, in a square cap and black gown, leaning on a stick, came out of it. Stead, after the respectful fashion of his earlier days, put his knee to the ground, doffed his steeple-crowned hat and craved a blessing, both he and the Doctor casting a quick glance round so as to be sure there was no one in sight.

Dr. Eales gave it earnestly, as one to whom it was a rare joy to find a country youth thus demanding it, and as he looked at the honest face he said:

"You are mine hostess' good purveyor, methinks, to whom I have often owed a wholesome meal."

"Steadfast Kenton, so please your reverence. There is a secret matter on which I would fain have your counsel, and Mistress Lightfoot thought I might speak to you here with greater safety."

"She did well. Speak on, my good boy, if we walk up and down here we shall be private. It does my heart good to commune with a faithful young son of the Church."

Steadfast told his story, at which the good old Canon was much affected. His brother Holworth, as he called him, was not in prison but in the Virginian plantations. He was still the only true minister of Elmwood, and Mr. Woodley, though owned by the present so-called law of the land, was not there rightly by the law of the Church, and, therefore, Stead was certainly not bound to surrender the trust to him, but rather the contrary.

The Doctor could have gone into a long disquisition about Presbyterian Orders, contradicting the arguments many good and devout people adduced in favour of them, but there was little time, so he only confirmed with authority Stead's belief that a Bishop's Ordination was indispensable to a true pastor, "the only door by which to enter to the charge of the fold."

Then came the other question of attendance on his ministry, and whether to attend the feast given out for the Sunday week, after the long-forced abstinence: Patience's, ever since the break-up of the parish; Steadfast's, since the siege of Bristol. Dr. Eales considered, "I cannot bid you go to that in the efficacy of which neither you nor I believe, my son," he said. "It would not be with faith. Here, indeed, I have ministered privately to a few of the faithful in their own houses, but the risk is over great for you and your sister to join us, espied as we are. How is it with your home?"

"O, sir, would you even come thither?" exclaimed Steadfast, joyfully, and he described his ravine, which was of course known to the Elmwood neighbours, but very seldom visited by them, never except in the middle of the day, and where the thicket and the caverns afforded every facility for concealment.

Whitsun Day was coming, and Dr. Eales proposed to come over to the glen and celebrate the Holy Feast in the very early morning before anyone was astir. There were a few of his Bristol flock who would be thankful for the opportunity of meeting more safely than they could do in the city, since at Easter they had as nearly as possible been all arrested in a pavilion in Mr. Rivett's garden which they had thought unsuspected.

There would be one market day first, and on that Stead would come and explain his preparations, and hear what the Doctor had arranged. And so it was. The time was to be three o'clock, the very dawn of the long summer day, the time when sleep is deepest. Dr. Eales and Mrs. Lightfoot would come out the night before, he not returning after his lesson to the Rivetts, and she making some excuse about going to see friends for the Sunday.

The Rivetts, living outside the gates where sentries still kept guard, could start in the morning, and so could the four others who were to form part of the congregation. Goody Grace was the only person near home whom Patience wished to invite, for she too had grieved over the great deprivation, and had too much heart for the Church to be satisfied with Mr. Woodley's ministrations. Perhaps even she did not understand the difference, but she could be trusted, and the young people knew how happy it would make her.

Little can we guess what such an opportunity was to the faithful children of the Church in those sad days. Goody Grace folded her hands and murmured, "Lord, now lettest Thou Thy servant depart in peace," when Patience told her of the invitation, and Patience, though she had all her ordinary work to do, went quietly about it, as if she had some great thought of peace and awe upon her.

"Why, Patience, you seem as if you were making ready for some guest, the Prince of Wales at least!" said Emlyn, on Saturday night.

Patience smiled a sweet little happy smile and in her heart she said "And so I am, and for a greater far!" but she did say "Yes, Emlyn, Dr. Eales is coming to sleep here to-night, and he will pray with us in the early morning."

It had been agreed that the Celebration should take place first, and then after a short pause, the Morning Service. Jerusha was eleven years old, and a very good girl, and since Confirmation was impossible, her brother and sister would have asked for her admission to the Holy Feast without it, but she could not be called up without the danger of awaking Emlyn; and Patience was so sure that it was not safe to trust that damsel with the full knowledge of the treasure that, though Steadfast always thought his sister hard on her, he was forced to give way. The children were to be admitted to Matins, for if any idea oozed out that this latter service had been held, no great danger was likely to come of it. Dr. Eales arrived in the evening, Steadfast meeting him to act as guide, and Patience set before him of her best. A fowl, which she had been forced to broil for want of other means of dressing it; bread baked in a tin with a fire of leaves and small sticks heaped over it; roasted eggs, excellent butter and milk. She apologised for not having dared to fetch any ale for fear of exciting suspicion, but the doctor set her quite at ease by his manifest enjoyment of her little feast, declaring that he had not made so good a meal since Bristol was taken.

Then he catechised the children. Little Ben could say the Lord's Prayer, the Belief, and some of the shorter Commandments, and the doctor patted his little round white cap, and gave him two Turkey figs as a reward.

Jerusha, when she got over her desperate fright enough to speak above a whisper, was quite perfect from her name down to "charity with all men," but Emlyn stumbled horribly over even the first answers, and utterly broke down in the Fourth Commandment; but she smiled up in the doctor's face in her pretty way, and blushed as she said "The chaplain at Blythedale had taught us so far, your reverence."

"And have you learnt no further?"

"If you were here to teach me, sir, I would soon learn it," said the little witch, but she did not come over him as she did with most people.

"You have as good an instructor as I for your needs, in this discreet maiden," said Dr. Eales, and as something of a pout descended on the sparkling little face, "when you know all the answers, perchance Steadfast here may bring you to my lodgings and I will hear you."

"I could learn them myself if I had the book," said Emlyn.

The fact being that the Catechism was taught by Patience from memory in those winter evenings when all went to bed to save candle light, but that when Steadfast retired to the cow-house, Emlyn either insisted on playing with the others or pretended to go to sleep; and twitted Patience with being a Puritan. However, the hopes of going into Bristol might be an incentive, though she indulged in a grumble to Rusha, and declared that she liked a jolly chaplain, and this old doctor was not a bit better than a mere Puritan.

Rusha opened her big eyes. She never did understand Emlyn, and perhaps that young maiden took delight in shocking her. They were ordered off to bed much sooner than they approved on that fair summer night, when the half-moon was high and the nightingales were singing all round—not that they cared for that, but there was a sense about them that something mysterious was going on, and Emlyn was wild with curiosity and vexation at being kept out of it.

She would have kept watch and crept out; but that Patience came in, and lay down, so close to the door that it was impossible to get out without waking her, and besides if Emlyn did but stir, she asked what was the matter.

"They mean something!" said Emlyn to herself, "and I'll know what it is. They have no right to keep me out of the plot; I am not like stupid little Rusha! I have been in a siege, and four battles, besides skirmishes! I'll watch till they think I'm asleep, if I pull all the hulls out of my bed! Then they will begin."

But nothing moved that Emlyn could hear or see. She woke and slept, but was quite aware when Patience rose up after a brief doze, and found the first streaks of dawn in the sky, a cuckoo calling as if for very life in the nearest tree, and Steadfast quietly sweeping the dew from the grass in a little open space shut in by rocks, trees, and bushes, close to the bank of the brook.

A chest which he kept in the cow-shed, and which bore traces of the fire in the old house, had been brought down to serve as an Altar, and it was laid over, for want of anything better, with one of poor Mrs. Kenton's best table-cloths, which Patience had always thought too good for use.

The next thing was to meet the rest of the scanty congregation at the entrances of the wood, and guide them to the spot. This was safely done, Goody Grace knew the way, and had guided one of the old Elmwood maid servants whom she had managed to shelter for the night. Mrs. Lightfoot was there with Mrs. Rivett, her daughter, elder son, and a grave-looking man servant, Mr. Henshaw, a Barbados merchant, with his wife, and a very worn battered shabby personage, but unmistakably a gentleman of quality, and wounded in the wars, for he was so lame that the merchant had to help him over the rough paths.

It was a wonderful Whitsun-day morning that none of the little party could ever forget. The sunrise could not be seen in that deep, narrow place, but the sky was of a strange pale shining blue, and the tender young green of the trees overhead was touched with gold, the glades of the wood were intensely blue with hyacinths, and with all sorts of delicate greens twined above in the bushes over them. A wild cherry, all silver white, was behind their Altar, the green floor was marbled with cuckoo flowers and buttercups, and the clear little stream whose voice murmured by was fringed with kingcups and forget-me-nots. The scents were of the most delicious dewy freshness; and as to the sounds! Larks sang high up in the sky, wood pigeons cooed around, nightingales, thrushes, every bird of the wood seemed to be trying to make music and melody.

And in the midst the grey-haired priest stood close to an ivy-covered rock, with the white covered Altar, and the bright golden vessels which he had carefully looked to in the night, and the little congregation knelt close round him on cloaks and mats, the women hooded, the old Cavalier's long thin locks, the merchant's dark ones, and the close cropped heads of the servant and of Steadfast bared to the morning breeze in its pure, dewy, soft freshness, fit emblem of the Comforter. No book was produced, all was repeated from memory. They durst not raise their voices, but the birds were their choir, and as they murmured their *Gloria in Excelsis*, the sweet notes rang out in that unconscious praise.

When the blessing of peace had been given there was a long hush, and no one rose till after the vessels had been replaced in their casket, and Stead was climbing up with it again to the hiding place. Then there was a move to the front of the hut, where Rusha was just awakening, and Emlyn feigned to be still asleep. It was not yet four o'clock, but the sweet freshness was still around everything. Young Mistress Alice Rivett and her brother were enchanted to gather flowers, and ran after their hosts to see the cows milked, and the goats, pigs, and poultry fed, sights new to them; but the elder ladies shivered and were glad to warm themselves at the little fire Patience hastily lighted, after cleaning the hut as fast as she could, by rolling up the bedding, and fairly carrying Ben out to finish his night's rest in the cow-house.

The guests had brought their provisions, and insisted that their young hosts should eat with them, accepting only the warm milk that Patience brought in her pail, and they drank from the horn cups of the family. Dr. Eales observed to the Cavalier that it was a true *Agape* or love-feast like those of the ancient Church, and the gentleman's melancholy, weather-beaten face relaxed into a smile as he sighed and hoped that the same endurance as that of the Christians of old would be granted in this time of persecution.

Emlyn was gratified at being a good deal noticed by the company as so unlike the others. She was not shy and frightened like Rusha, who hung her head and had not a word to say for herself, but chattered away to the young Rivetts, showing them the kid, the calves, and the lambs, taking Mistress Alice to the biggest cowslips and earliest wild roses, and herself making a sweet posy for each of the ladies. The old Cavalier himself, Colonel Harford, was even amused with the pretty little maid, who, he told Dr. Eales, resembled Mirth as Master John Milton had depicted her, ere he took up with General Cromwell and his crew; and was a becoming figure for this early morn.

On learning the child's history, he turned out to know Sir Harry Blythedale, but not to have heard of him since they had parted at Newark, he to guard the king to Oxford, Sir Harry to join Lord Astley, and he much feared that the old knight had been killed at Stowe, in the fight between Astley and Brereton. This would account for nothing having been heard from him about Emlyn, but Colonel Harford promised, if any opportunity should offer, to communicate with Lady Blythedale, whom he believed to be living at Worcester; and he patted Emlyn on the head, called her a little loyal veteran, accepted a tiny posy of forget-me-not from her, and after fumbling in his pocket, gave her a crown piece. Steadfast and Patience were afraid it was his last, and much wished she had contrived not to take it, but she said she should keep it for a remembrance.

After this rest, the beautiful Whitsuntide Matins was said in the fair forest church, and before six o'clock this strange and blessed festival had ended, though not the peace and thankfulness in the hearts of the little flock.

Indeed, instead of a sermon, Dr. Eales's parting words were "And he went in the strength of that meat forty days and forty nights."

CHAPTER XVI

A FAIR OFFER

"We be content," the keepers said,
"We three and you no less,
Then why should we of you be afraid,
As we never did transgress."
ROBIN HOOD BALLAD.

Steadfast was busy weeding the little patch of barley that lay near the ruins of the old farm house with little Ben basking round him. The great carefulness as to keeping the ground clear had been taught him by his father, and was one reason why his fields, though so small, did not often bear a bad crop. He heard his name called over the hedge, and looking up saw the Squire, Mr. Elmwood, on horseback.

He came up, respectfully taking off his hat and standing with it in his hand as was then the custom when thus spoken to. "What is this I hear, Kenton," said the squire, "that you have been having a prelatist service on your ground?"

Steadfast was dismayed, but did not speak, till Mr. Elmwood added, "Is it true?"

"Yes, sir," he answered resolutely.

"Did you know it was against the law to use the Book of Common Prayer?"

"There was no book, sir."

"But you do not deny it was the same superstitious and Popish ceremony and festival abolished by law."

"No, sir," Stead allowed, though rather by gesture than word.

"Now, look you here, young Kenton, I ask no questions. I do not want to bring anyone into trouble, and you are a hard-working, honest lad by what they tell me, who have a brother fighting in the good Cause and have suffered from the lawless malignants yourself. Was it not the Prince's troopers that wrought this ruin?" pointing towards the blackened gable, "and shot down your father? Aye! The more shame you should hold with them! I wish you no harm I say, nor the blinded folk who must have abused your simplicity: but I am a justice of the peace, and I will not have laws broken on my land. If this thing should happen again, I shall remember that you have no regular or lawful tenure of this holding, and put you forth from it."

He waited, but a threat always made silent resistance easy to Steadfast, and there was no answer.

Mr. Elmwood, however, let that pass, for he was not a hard or a fanatical man, and he knew that to hold such a service was not such an easy matter that it was likely to be soon repeated. He looked round at the well-mended fences, the clean ground, and the tokens of intelligent industry around, and the clean homespun shirt sleeves that spoke of the notable manager at home. "You are an industrious fellow, my good lad," he said, "how long have you had this farm to yourself?"

"Getting on for five years, your honour," said Steadfast.

"And is that your brother?"

"Yes, please your honour," picking Ben up in his arms to prevent the barley from being pulled up by way of helping him.

"How many of you are there?"

"Five of us, sir, but my eldest brother is in Captain Venn's troop."

"So I heard, and what is this about a child besides?"

"An orphan, sir, I found after the skirmish at the mill stream, who was left with us till her friends can send after her."

"Well, well. You seem a worthy youth," said Mr. Elmwood, who was certainly struck and touched by the silent uncomplaining resolution of the mere stripling who had borne so heavy a burthen. "If you were heartily one of us, I should be glad to make you woodward, instead of old Tomkins, and build up yonder house for you, but I cannot do it for one who is hankering after prelacy, and might use the place for I know not what plots and conspiracies of the malignants."

Again Steadfast took refuge in a little bow of acknowledgment, but kept his lips shut, till again the squire demanded, "What do you think of it? There's a fair offer. What have you to say for yourself?"

He had collected himself and answered, "I thank you, sir. You are very good. If you made me woodward, I would serve your honour faithfully, and have no plots or the like there. But, your honour, I was bred up in the Church and I cannot sell myself."

"Why, you foolish, self-conceited boy, what do you know about it? Is not what is good enough for better men than you fit to please you?"

To this Stead again made no answer, having said a great deal for him.

"Well," said Mr. Elmwood, angered at last, "if ever I saw a dogged moon-calf, you are one! However, I let you go scot free this time, in regard for your brother's good service, and the long family on your hands, but mind, I shall put in an active woodward instead of old Tomkins, who has been past his work these ten years, and if ever I hear of seditious or prelatical doings in yonder gulley again, off you go."

He rode off, leaving Steadfast with temper more determined, but mind not more at ease. The appointment of a woodward was bad news, for the copsewood and the game had been left to their fate for the last few years, and what were the rights of the landlord over them Stead did not know, so that there might be many causes of trouble, especially if the said woodward considered him a person to be specially watched. Indeed, the existence of such a person would make a renewal of what Mr. Elmwood called the prelatist assembly impossible, and with a good deal of sorrow he announced the fact on the next market day to Mrs. Lightfoot. He could not see Dr. Eales, but when next he came in, she gave him paper on which was simply marked "Ps. xxxvii, 7." He looked out the reference and found "Hold thee still in the Lord and abide patiently upon Him." Stead hoped that Patience and the rest would never know what an offer had been made to him, but Master Brown, who had recommended him, and who did not at all like the prospect of a strange woodward, came to expostulate with him for throwing away such a chance for a mere whim, telling Patience she was a sensible wench and ought to persuade her brother to see what was for his own good and the good of all, holding up himself as an example.

"I never missed my church and had the parson's good word all along, and yet you see I am ready to put up with this good man without setting myself up to know more than my elders and betters! Eh! Hast not a word to say for thyself? Then I'll tell the squire, who is a good and friendly gentleman to all the old servants, that you have thought better of it, and will thankfully take his kindness, and do your best."

"I cannot go against father," said Steadfast.

"And what would he have done, good man, but obey them that have the rule, and let wiser folk think for thee. But all the young ones are pig-headed as mules now-a-days, and must think for themselves, one running off to the Independents, and one to the Quakers and Shakers, and one to the Fifth Monarchy men, and you, Steadfast Kenton, that I thought better things of, talking of the Church and offending the squire with thy prelatic doings, that have been forbidden by Act of Parliament. What say you to that, my lad? Come, out with it," for Stead had more difficulty in answering Master Brown, who had been a great authority throughout his life, than even the Squire himself.

"Parson said there was higher law than Parliament."

"Eh! What, the King? He is a prisoner, bless him, but they will never let him go till they have bent him to their will, and what will you do then?"

"Not the King," muttered Steadfast.

"Eh! what! If you have come to pretending to know the law of God better than your elders, you are like the rest of them, and I have done with you." And away tramped the steward in great displeasure, while Patience put her apron over her head and cried bitterly.

She supposed Stead might be right, but what would it not have been to have the old house built up, and all decent about them as it was in mother's time, and fit places to sleep in, now that the wenches were growing bigger?

"But you know, Patty, we are saving for that."

"Aye, and how long will it take? And now this pestilent woodward will be always finding fault—killing the fowls and ducks, and seizing the swine and sheep, and very like slaughtering the dogs and getting us turned out of house and home; for now you have offended the squire, he will believe anything against us."

"Come, Patty, you know I could not help it. This is sorest of all, you that have always stood by me and father's wish."

"Yes, yes," sobbed Patience. "I wot you are right, Stead. I'll hold to you, though I wish—I wish you would think like other folk."

Yet Patience knew in her secret soul that then he would not be her own Steadfast, and she persuaded him no more, though the discomforts and deficiencies of their present home tried her more and more as the family grew older. Stead had contrived a lean-to, with timbers from the old house, and wattled sides stuffed with moss, where he and little Ben slept in summer time, and they had bought or made some furniture—a chair and table, some stools, bedding, and kitchen utensils, and she toiled to keep things clean, but still it was a mere hovel, with the door opening out into the glade. Foxes and polecats prowled, owls hooted, and the big dog outside was a needful defender, even in summer time, and in winter the cold was piteous, the wet even worse, and they often lost some of their precious animals—chickens died of cold, and once three lambs had been carried away in a sudden freshet. Yet Patience, when she saw Steadfast convinced, made up her mind to stand by him, and defended him when the younger girls murmured.

Rusha was of a quiet, acquiescent, contented nature, and said little, as Emlyn declared, "She knew nothing better;" but Emlyn was more and more weary of the gulley, and as nothing was heard of her friends, and she was completely one of the home, she struggled more with the dullness and loneliness. She undertook all errands to the village for the sake of such change as a chatter with the young folk there afforded her, or for the chance of seeing the squire's lady or sons and daughters go by; and she was wild to go on market days to Bristol.

In spite of Puritan greyness, soldiers, sailors, gentlemen, ladies, and even fashions, such as they were, could be seen there, and news picked up, and Emlyn would fain have persuaded Steadfast that she should be the most perfect market woman, if he would only let her ride in on the donkey between the panniers, in a broad hat, with chickens and ducks dangling round, eggs, butter, and fruit or nuts, and even posies, according to the season, and sit on the steps of the market-place among the other market women and girls.

Steadfast would have been the last to declare that her laughing dark eyes, and smiling lips, and arch countenance would not bring many a customer, but he knew well that his mother would never have sent his sister to be thus exposed, and he let her pout, or laughed away her refusal by telling her that he was bound not to let a butler's daughter demean herself to be stared at by all the common folk, who would cheapen her wares.

And when she did coax him to take her to Bristol on any errand she could invent, to sell her yarns, or buy pins, or even a ribbon, he was inexorable in leaving her under Mrs. Lightfoot's care, and she had to submit, even though it sometimes involved saying her catechism to Dr. Eales. Yet that always ended in the old man's petting her. It was only from her chatter that the old clergyman ever knew of the proposal that Stead had rejected for conscience's sake. It vexed the lad so much that he really could not bear to think of it, and it would come over him now and then, was it all for nothing? Would the Church ever lift up her head again? or would Mr. Woodley be always in possession at Elmwood Church, where everyone seemed to be content with him. The Kentons went thither. It was hardly safe to abstain, for a fine upon absence was still the law of the land, though seldom enforced; and Dr. Eales who considered Presbyterianism by far the least unorthodox and most justifiable sect, had advised Stead not to allow himself or the others altogether to lose the habit of public worship, but to abstain from Communions which might be an act of separation from the Church, and which could not be accepted by her children as genuine. Such was the advice of most of the divines of the English Church in this time of eclipse; and though Stead, and still less Patience, did not altogether follow the reasoning, they obeyed, while aware that they incurred suspicion from the squire by not coming to "the table."

The new woodward, Peter Pierce, was not one of the villagers as usual, but had been a soldier in one of the regiments of the Earl of Essex, in which Mr. Elmwood's eldest son had served.

Instead of succeeding to old Tomkins's lodge in the great wood, he had a new one built for him, so as to command the opening of Hermit's Gulley towards the village, and one of the Bristol roads. Could this be for the sake of watching over anything so insignificant as the Kentons?

The copse on their side of the brook was their own, free to do what they chose with except cutting down the timber trees, but the further side was the landlord's, as they had now to remember; and as, when the brook was at its lowest, their pigs and goats were by no means likely to recollect; though Steadfast was extremely anxious to give no occasion for the mistrust and ill-will with which Pierce regarded him, as a squatter, trespasser, and poacher, almost as a matter of course, and likewise a prelatist and plotter.

Once he did find a kid on the wrong side, standing on a rock, browsing a honeysuckle, and was about either to seize it or shoot it, as it went off in three bounds, when Emlyn darted out, and threw herself between. It was her darling kid, it should never trespass again, she would—she would thank him ever more—if he would spare it this once.

And Emlyn as usual had touched the soft place in the heart of even a woodward. He told her not to cry, and contented himself with growling a tremendous warning to Steadfast and Patience.

There were several breezes about Growler, who was only too apt to use his liberty in pursuing rabbits on the wrong side, and whom Peter more than once condemned; but Emlyn and Ben begged him off, and he was kept well chained up. At last, however, he won even the woodward's favour by the slaughter of a terrible wild cat and her brood, after all Peter's dogs had returned with bleeding faces from the combat.

The woodward had another soft place in his heart. He had a pretty young wife and a little son. Nanny Pierce was older in years, but far more childish than Patience, and the life in this gulley seemed to her utter solitude and desolation, and if Patience had been ten times a poacher and a prelatist, she could not have helped making friends with the only creature of her own kind within a mile. And when Patience's experience with Ben and other older babes at rest in the churchyard, had aided the poor little helpless woman through a convulsion fit of her baby's before Goody Grace could arrive, Peter himself owned that "the Kenton wench was good for somewhat," though he continued to think Steadfast's great carefulness not to transgress, only a further proof that "he was a deep one"—all the more because he refused to let anyone but himself have a search for a vanished polecat in "them holes," which Peter was persuaded contained some mystery, though Steadfast laid it, and not untruly, on the health of the young stock he kept penned in the caves, which were all, he hoped, of which Peter was aware.

All this was harassing, but a greater trouble came in the second winter. Good Dr. Eales was failing, and the tidings of the King's execution were a blow that he never recovered. Mrs. Lightfoot had tears in her eyes when Stead asked after him, week by week, and she could only say that he was feebler, and spent all his days in prayer—often with tears.

At last came peace. He lay still and calm, and sent a message that young Kenton should be brought to him for a last farewell.

And as Stead stood sorrowful and awed by his bed side, he bade the youth never despair or fall away from his hope of the restoration of the Church.

"Remember," he said, "she is founded on a rock, and the gates of hell shall never prevail against her. She shall stand forth for evermore as the moon, which wanes but to wax again; and I have good hope that thou wilt see it, my son. He that shall endure unto the end, the same shall be saved."

Then Dr. Eales pointed to a small parcel of books, which he had caused Mrs. Lightfoot to put together, telling Steadfast that he had selected them alike for devotion and for edification, and that if he studied them, he would have no doubt when he might deliver up his trust to a true priest of the Church.

"And if none should return in my time?" asked Steadfast.

"Have I not told thee never to despair of God's care for His Church? Yet His time is not as our time, and it may be—that young as thou art—the days of renewal may not be when thou shalt see them. Should it thus be, my son, leave the secret with one whom thou canst securely trust. Better the sacred vessels should lie hidden than that thou shouldst show thy faith wanting by surrendering them to any, save according to the terms of thy vow. See, Steadfast, among these books is a lighter one, a romance of King Arthur, that I loved well in my boyhood, and which may not only serve thee as fair pastime in the winter nights, but will mind thee of thine high and holy charge, for it goeth deeper than the mere outside."

His voice was growing weak. Mrs. Lightfoot gave him a cordial, and Stead knelt by his bedside, felt his hand on his head, and heard his blessing for the last time. The next market day, when he called at the good bakester's stall, she told him in floods of tears that the guest who had brought a blessing on her house, was gone to his rest.

CHAPTER XVII

THE GROOM IN GREY

"Heroes and kings, in exile forced to roam,
Leave swelling phrase and seven-leagued words at home."
                        SCOTT.

Another summer and winter had gone by and harvest time had come again, when Steadfast with little Ben, now seven years old, for company, took two sacks of corn to be ground at the mill, where the skirmish had been fought in which Emlyn's father had been killed.

The sacks were laid across a packsaddle on a stout white horse, with which, by diligent saving, Steadfast had contrived to replace Whitefoot, Ben was promised a ride home when the sacks should have been emptied, and trotted along in company with Growler by his brother's side, talking more in an hour than Stead did in a week, and looking with great interest to be shown the hawthorn bush where Emlyn had been found. For Stead and Ben were alike in feeling the bright, merry, capricious, laughing, teasing Emlyn the charm and delight of home. In trouble, or for real aid, they went to Patience, but who was like Emlyn for drollery and diversion? Who ever made Stead laugh as she could, or who so played with Ben, and never, like Rusha, tried to be maidenly, discreet, nay, dull?

It was very inconvenient that just as they reached the famous thorn bush, the white horse began to demonstrate that his shoe was loose. They were very near the mill, and after disposing of the sacks, the brothers led the horse on to a forge, about a furlong beyond. It was not a place of which Stead was fond, as the smith was known to be strong for the Covenant, and he could not help wishing that the shoe had come off nearer to his good friend Smith Blane.

Original-Sin Hopkins, which was the name of the blacksmith, was in great excitement, as he talked of the crowning mercy vouchsafed at Worcester, and how the son of the late man, Charles Stewart, had been utterly defeated, and his people scattered like sheep without a shepherd. Three or four neighbours were standing about, listening to the tidings he had heard from a messenger on the way to Bristol. One was leaning on the unglazed window frame, and a couple of old men basking, even in that September day, in the glow of the fire, while a few women and children loitered around, thinking it rather fine to hear Master Original-Sin declaim on the backsliding of the Scots in upholding the son of the oppressor.

The shoeing of Stead Kenton's horse seemed a trivial matter beneath the attention of such an orator; but he vouchsafed to bid his lad drive in a few nails; and just as the task was commenced, there came to the forge a lady in a camlet riding dress and black silk hood, walking beside a stout horse, which a groom was leading with great care, for it had evidently lost a shoe. And it had a saddle with a pillion on which they had been riding double, after the usual fashion of travelling for young and healthy gentlewomen in those days of bad roads.

The lady, a quiet, self-possessed person, not in her first youth, came forward, and in the first pause in the blacksmith's declamation, begged that he would attend to her horse.

He gave a nod as if intending her to wait till Steadfast's work was done, and went on. "And has it not been already brought about that the man of blood hath—"

"So please you," interrupted the lady, "to shoe my horse at once. I am on my way to Abbotsleigh, and my cousin, Mr. Norton, knows that my business brooks no delay."

Mr. Norton, though a Royalist, was still the chief personage in that neighbourhood, and his name produced sufficient effect on Original-Sin to make him come forward, look at the hoof, and select a shoe from those hung on the walls of his forge. Little Ben looked on, highly delighted to watch the proceedings, and Steadfast, as he waited, glanced towards the servant, a well-made young man, in a trim, sober suit of grey cloth, with a hat a good deal slouched over a dark swarthy face, that struck Stead as having been seen by him before.

After all, the lady's horse was the first finished. Hopkins looked at all the other three shoes, tapped them with his hammer, and found them secure, received the money from the lady, but gave very slight salutations as the pair remounted, and rode away.

Then he twisted up his features and observed, "Here is a dispensation! As I am a living soul, this horse shoe was made at Worcester. I know the make. My cousin was apprenticed there."

"Well, outlandish work goes against one's stomach," said one of the bystanders, "but what of that, man?"

"Seest thou not, Jabez Holt? Is not the young man there one of them who trouble Israel, and the lady is striving for his escape. Mr. Norton is well known as a malignant at heart, and his man Pope hath been to and fro these last days as though evil were being concerted. I would that good Master Hatcham were here."

"Poor lad. Let him alone. 'Tis hard he should not get off," said one of the bystanders.

"I tell thee he is one of the brood of Satan, who have endeavoured to break up the godly peace of the saints, and fill this goodly land with blood and fire. Is it not said 'Root them out that they be no more a people?'"

"Have after them, then," said another of the company. "We want no more wars, to be taking our cows and killing our pigs. After them, I say!"

"You haven't got no warrant, 'Riginal," said a more cautious old man. "Best be on the safe side. Go after constable first, and raise the hue-and-cry. You'll easy overtake them. Breakneck Hill be sore for horseflesh."

"I'd fain see Master Hatcham," said the smith, scratching his head.

Stead had meantime been listening as he paid his pence. It flashed over him now where he had beheld those intensely dark eyes, and the very peculiar cut of features, though they had then been much more boyish. It was when he had seen the Prince of Wales going to the Cathedral on Christmas Day, in the midst of all his plumed generals, with their gay scarfs, and rich lace collars.

He had put little Ben on horseback, and turned away into the long, dirty lane, or rather ditch, that led homeward, before, through his consternation, there dawned on him what to do. A gap in the hedge lay near, through which he dragged the horse into a pasture field, to the great amazement of Ben, saying "See here, Ben, those folk want to take yonder groom in grey. We will go and warn them."

Ben heartily assented.

"I like the groom," he said. "He jumped me five times off the horseblock, and he patted Growler and called him a fine fellow, who didn't deserve his name—worth his salt he was sure. We won't give Growler salt, Stead, but don't let that ugly preaching man get the good groom!"

Steadfast was by this time on the horse behind his little brother, pressing through the fields, which by ancient custom were all thrown open from harvest time till Christmas; and coming out into the open bit of common that the travellers had to pass before arriving at Breakneck Hill, he was just in time to meet them as they trotted on. He hardly knew what he said, as he doffed his hat, and exclaimed—

"Madam, you are pursued."

"Pursued!" Both at once looked back.

"There's time," said Steadfast; "but Smith Hopkins said one of the shoes was Worcester make, and he is gone to fetch the constable and raise the hue-and-cry."

"And you are a loyal—I mean an honest lad—come to warn us," said the groom.

"Yes, sir. I think, if you will trust me, they can be put off the track."

"Trusty! Your face answers for you. Eh, fair Mistress Jane?"

"Sir, it must be as you will."

"This way then, sir," said Steadfast, who was off his own horse by this time, and leading it into a rough track through a thicket whence some timber had been drawn out in the summer.

"They will see where we turned off," whispered the lady.

"No, ma'am, not unless you get off the hard ground. Besides they will go on the way to Breakneck Hill. Hark! I hear a hallooing. Not near—no—no fear, madam."

They were by this time actually hidden from the common by the copsewood, and the distant shouts of the hue-and-cry kept all silent till they were fairly out beyond it, not far from Stead's own fields.

Happily they had hitherto met no one, but there was danger now of encountering gleaners, and indeed Stead's white horse could be seen from a distance, and might attract attention to his companions.

"Hallo!" exclaimed the groom, as they halted under shelter of a pollard willow. "I've heard tell that a white horse is the surest mark for a bullet in a battle, and if that be Breakneck Hill, as you call it, your beast may bring the sapient smith down on us. Had we not best part?"

"Aye," said Steadfast. "I was thinking what was best. Whither were you going?"

He blurted it out, not knowing to whom to address himself, or how to frame his speech. The lady hesitated, but her companion named Castle Carey.

"Then, please your honour," said Stead, impartially addressing both, "methinks the best course would be, if this—"

"Groom William," suggested that personage.

"Would go down into yonder covert with my little brother here, where my poor place is, and where my sister can show a safe hiding-place, in case Master Hopkins suspects me, and follows; but I scarce think he will. Then meanwhile, if the lady will trust herself to me—"

"O! there is no danger for me," she said.

"Go on, my Somerset Solomon," said the groom.

"Then would I take the lady on for a short space to a good woman in Elmwood there. And on the way this horse shall lose his Worcester shoe, and I will get Smith Blane, who is an honest fellow, to put on another; and when the chase is like to be over, I will come back for him and put you on the cross lane for Castle Carey, which don't join with the road you came by, till just ere you get into the town."

"There's wit as well as cheese in Somerset. What say you, my guardian angel?" said Groom William.

"It sounds well," she reluctantly answered. "Does Mr. Norton know you, young man?"

"No, madam," said Stead, with much stumbling. "But I have seen him in Bristol. My Lady Elmwood knew of me, and Sir George Elmwood too, and the Dean could say I was honest."

"Which the face of you says better than your tongue," said the groom. "Have with you then, my bold little elf," he added, taking the bridle of the horse on which Ben was still seated. "Or one moment more. You knew me, my lad— are there any others like to do so?"

"I had seen you, sir, at Bristol, and that is why I would not have you shew yourself in Elmwood. But my sister has never seen you, and the only neighbours who ever come in are the woodward and his wife. He served in my Lord of Essex's army, but he has never seen you. Moreover, he was to be at the squire's to-day helping to stack his corn. Ben, do you tell Patience that *he*"—again taking refuge in a pronoun—"is a gentleman in danger, and she must see to his safety for an hour or two till I come back for him."

"A gentleman in danger," repeated Ben, anxious to learn his lesson.

"He and I will take care of that," said the grey-coated groom gaily, as he turned the horse's head, and waved his hat in courtly fashion to the lady so that Steadfast saw that his hair was cropped into black stubble.

"Ah!" said the lady with a sigh, for the loss of a Cavalier's locks was a dreadful thing. "You know him then."

"I have seen him at Bristol," said Steadfast, with considerably less embarrassment, though still in the clownish way he could not shake off.

"And you know how great is the trust you—nay, we have undertaken. But, as he says, he has learnt the true fidelity of a leathern jerkin."

Then Jane Lane told Steadfast of the King's flight from Worcester, and adventures at Boscobel with the Penderells, and how she had brought him to Abbotsleigh, in hopes of finding a ship at Bristol, but that failing, it was too perilous for him to remain there, so that she was helping him as far as Castle Carey on his way to Trent.

Before they were clear of the wood, Stead asked her to pause. He knocked off the tell-tale shoe with the help of a stone, threw it away into the middle of a bramble, and then after a little consultation, she decided on herself encountering the smith, not perhaps having much confidence in the readiness of speech or invention of her companion.

When they arrived at the forge, where good-humoured, brawny Harry Blane was no small contrast to his gaunt compeer Original-Sin Hopkins, she averred that she was travelling from her relations, and having been obliged to send her servant back for a packet that had been forgotten, this good youth, who had come to her help when her horse had cast a shoe, had undertaken to guide her to the smith's, and to take her again to meet her man, if he did not come for her himself. Might she be allowed in the meantime to sit with Master Blane's good housewife?

Master Blane was only too happy, and Mistress Jane Lane was accordingly introduced to the pleasant kitchen, with sanded floor, and big oak table, open hearth, and beaupots in the oriel window where the spinning-wheel stood, and where the neat and hospitable Dame Blane made her kindly welcome.

Steadfast, marvelling at her facility of speech, and glad the king's safety did not depend on his uttering such a story, told Blane that he must go after his cattle and should look after the groom on the way.

As he walked through the wood, and drew near the glade, he was dismayed to hear voices, and to see Peter Pierce leaning against the wall of the house, but Rusha came running up to him exclaiming, "Oh! Stead, here is this good stranger that you met, telling us all about brother Jeph."

"Yes, my kind host," said the grey-coated guest, with a slight nasal intonation, rising as Stead came near, "I find that you are the very lad my friend and brother Jephthah Kenton, that singular Christian man, bade me search out. 'If you go near Bristol, beloved,' quoth he,' search me out my brothers Steadfast and Benoni, and my sisters, Patience and Jerusha, and greet them well from me, and bear witness of me to them. They dwell, said he, in a lonely hut in the wood side, and with them a fair little maiden, sprung of the evil and idolatrous seed of the malignants, but whom their pious nurture may yet bring to a knowledge of the truth,' and by that token, I knew that it was the same." There was an odd little twinkle towards Emlyn just then.

"And Stead, Jeph is an officer," said Patience, who was busied in setting before the visitor on a little round table, the best ale, bread, cheese, and butter that her hut afforded, together with an onion, which, he declared, was "what his good grandfather, a valiant man for the godly, had ever loved best."

"An officer! Aye is he. A captain of his Ironside troop, very like to be Colonel ere long."

Stead was absolutely bewildered, and could not find speech, beyond an awkward "Where?"

"Where was he when I last saw him? Charging down the main street of Worcester, where the malignants and Charles Stewart made their last stand. Smiting them hip and thigh with the sword of Gedaliah, nay, my tongue tripped, 'twas Gideon I would say."

"Aye," said the woodward, "Squire had the tidings two days back in a news letter. It was a mighty victory of General Cromwell."

"In sooth it was," returned the groom; "and I hear he hath ordered a solemn thanksgiving therefore."

"But Jephthah," put in Patience, "you are sure he was not hurt?"

"The hand of Heaven protecteth the godly," again through his nose spoke the guest. "He was well when I left him; being sent south by my master to attend my mistress, and so being no more among them that divide the spoil."

"Where have you served, sir?" demanded the woodward.

"I am last from Scotland," was the answer. "A godly land!"

"Ah! I know nought of Scotland," said the woodward. "I was disbanded when my Lord Essex gave up the command, more's the pity, for he was for doing things soberly and reasonably, and ever in the name of the poor King that is gone! You look too young to have seen fire at Edgehill or Exeter, sir."

"Did I not?" said the youth. "Aye, I was with my father, though only as a boy apart on a hill."

The reminiscences that were exchanged astonished Steadfast beyond measure, and really made him doubt whether what had previously passed had not been all a dream. The language was so like Jephthah's own too, all except that one word "fair" applied to Emlyn; and Patience, Rusha, and the Pierces were entirely without a suspicion, that their guest was other than he seemed. How much must have been picked out of little Ben, without the child's knowing it, to make such acting possible?

And how was the woodward, who was so much delighted with the visitor, to be shaken off? Stead stood silent, puzzled, anxious, and wondering what to do next, a very heavy and awkward host, so that even Patience wondered what made him so shy.

Suddenly, however, a whistle, and the sharp yap of a dog was heard across the stream. Nanny Pierce exclaimed, "There are those rascal lads after the rabbits again!" and the gamekeeper's instinct awoke. Pierce shook hands with his fellow soldier, regretted he could not see more of him, and received his promise that if he came that way again, he would share a pottle of ale at the lodge; and then tramped off after his poachers over the stream.

Groom William then kissed the young women (the usual mode of salutation then), Nanny Pierce and all, thanked Patience, and looked about for the goodly little malignant, as he called Emlyn, but she was nowhere to be seen, and Stead hurried him off through the wood.

"Ho! ho! sly rascal," said Charles, as they turned away. "You're jealous! You would keep the game to yourself."

Stead had no answer to make to this banter, the very notion of Emlyn as aught but the orphan in his charge was new to him.

They were not yet beyond the gulley when from between the hazel stems, out sprang Emlyn, and kneeling on the ground caught the King's hand and kissed it.

"Fairy-haunted wood!" cried Charles, and indeed it was done with great natural grace, and the little figure with the glowing cheeks, her hood flying back so as to shew her brilliant eyes sparkling with delight and enthusiasm, was a truly charming vision. "It is like one of the masques of the merry days of old." And as he retained her hand and returned the salute on her lips, "Queen Mab herself, for who else saw through thy poor brother sovereign's mean disguise?"

"I had seen your Majesty with the army," replied Emlyn, modestly blushing a good deal.

"Ah! The Fates have provided me with a countenance the very worst for straits like mine. But that matters the less since it is only my worthy subjects who see through the grey coat. I would lay my crown, if I had it, to one of those crispy ringlets of yours, that Queen Mab was the poacher who drew off the crop-eared keeper."

"'Tis Robin Goodfellow, please your Majesty, who leads clowns astray," said Emlyn in the same tone.

"Sometimes a horse I'll be, sometimes a hound," quoted the King.

Stead could only listen in amazement without a word to say for himself. Near the confines of the wood, he had to leave Emlyn to guide the King over a field-path while he fetched Mrs. Jane Lane and the horse to meet them beyond, as it was wiser for the King not to shew himself in the village. Again Charles jested on his supposed jealousy of leaving the fair Queen Mab alone in such company, and on his blunt answer, "I only feared the saucy child might be troublesome, sir."

At which the King laughed the more, and even Emlyn smiled a little.

All was safely accomplished, and when Steadfast had brought Mrs. Lane to the deep lane, they found the King and Emlyn standing by the stile, and could hear the laughter of both as they approached.

"He can always thus while away his cares," said Jane Lane in quite a motherly tone. "And well it is that he is of so joyous a nature."

Perhaps it was said as a kind of excuse for the levity of one in so much danger chattering to the little woodland maid so mirthfully, and like one on an equality. When they appeared, Charles bestowed a kiss on Emlyn's lips, and shook hands cordially with Steadfast, lamenting that he had no reward, nor even a token to leave with them.

Stead made his rustic bow, pinched his hat, and muttered, "It is enough to—"

"Enough reward to have served your Majesty," said Emlyn, "he would say."

"Yea, and it is your business to find words for him, pretty one," said the King. "A wholesome partnership—eh? He finds worth, and you find wit! And so we leave the fairy buried in the woodland."

And on the wanderers rode, while Steadfast and Emlyn turned back over the path through the fields; and she eagerly told that the King had slept at Blythedale on his way to Worcester, and that though Sir Harry was dead, his son was living in Holland. "And if the King gets there safely, he will tell Master George, and if my uncle is with him, no doubt he will send for me, or mayhap, come and fetch me."

There was a shock of pain in Steadfast's heart.

"You would be glad?"

"Poor old Stead. I would scarce be glad to quit you. I doubt me if the Hague, as they call it, would show me any one I should care for as much as for your round shoulders, you good old lubber! But you should come too, and the King would give you high preferment, when he comes to his own again, and then we won't be buried alive in this Hermit's Gulley."

She danced about in exultation, hardly knowing what wild nonsense she talked, and Stead was obliged to check her sharply in an attempt to sing

"The king shall enjoy his own again."

"But Stead," asked Ben, after long reflection, "how could Groom William know all about brother Jeph?"

A question Stead would not hear, not wishing to destroy confidence in His Majesty's veracity.

CHAPTER XVIII

JEPH'S GOOD FORTUNE

"Still sun and rain made emerald green the loveliest fields on earth,
And gave the type of deathless hope, the little shamrock, birth."
IRISH BALLAD.

The King's visit left traces. Emlyn had become far more restless and consciously impatient of the dullness and seclusion of the Hermit's Gulley. Not only did she, as before, avail herself of every pretext for going into the village, or for making expeditions to Bristol, but she openly declared the place a mere grave, intolerable to live in, and she confided to Jerusha that the King had declared that it was a shame to hide her there—such charms were meant for the world.

The only way of getting into the world that occurred to her was going into service at Bristol, and she talked of this whenever she specially hated her spinning, or if Patience ventured to complain of her gadding about, gossiping with Nanny Pierce or Kitty Blane, or getting all the young lads in Elmwood round her, to be amused and teased by her lively rattle.

Patience began to be decidedly of opinion that it would be much better for all parties that the girl should be under a good mistress. Both she and Rusha were over sixteen years old; and though it was much improved, the house was hardly fit for so many inhabitants, and both Goody Grace and Dame Blane had told Patience that it would be better, both for the awkward Rusha and the gay Emlyn, if they could have some household training.

Mistress Elmwood, at the Hall, had noted the family at church, and observed their perfect cleanliness and orderliness, and it was intimated that at the Ladyday hiring, she would take Rusha among her maidens.

Shy Rusha cried a great deal, and wished Emlyn would go instead, but Mrs. Elmwood would not have hired that flighty damsel on any account, and Emlyn was sure it would be but mopish work to live under a starched old Puritan. Mrs. Lightfoot was therefore applied to, to find a service for Emlyn Gaythorn, and she presently discovered one Mistress Sloggett, a haberdasher's wife of wealth and consideration, who wanted a young maidservant.

Emlyn was presented to her by the bakester, undertook for everything, and was hired by the twelvemonth, going off in high glee at the variety and diversion she expected to enjoy at the sign of the "Sheep and Shears," though clinging with much tenderness to her friends as they parted.

"Remember, Emlyn, this is the home where you will always be welcome," said Stead.

"As if I wanted to *remember* it," said Emlyn, with her sweet smile. "As if I did not know where be kind hearts."

The hovel seemed greatly deserted when the two young girls were gone. Patience sorely missed Rusha, her diligent little helper, and latterly her companion too; and the lack of Emlyn's merry tongue made all around seem silent and tedious. Steadfast especially missed the girl. Perhaps it was due to the King's gibes that her absence fully opened to him the fact that he knew not how to do without her. After his usual fashion, he kept the discovery to himself, not even talking to Patience about it, being very shamefaced at the mere thought, which gave a delicious warmth to his heart, though it made him revolve schemes of saving up till he had a sufficient sum, with which to go to the squire and propose to meet him half-way in rebuilding the old house; not such an expensive matter as it would be in these days. There, in full view of all that passed down Elmwood Lane, Emlyn could not complain of solitude, he thought! But there was this difficulty in the way, that Jephthah had never resigned his claims as eldest son, and might come home at any time, and take possession of all the little farm at which Steadfast had worked for seven years.

The war was over, and nothing had been heard of Jeph, except the king's apocryphal history, since his visit after the taking of Bristol. Patience had begun to call him "poor Jeph," and thought he must have been killed, but Stead had ascertained that the army had not been disbanded, and believed him still to be employed.

At length, one market day, Mrs. Lightfoot told him, "There has been one asking for you, Kenton, Seth Coleman, the loriner's son, that went soldiering when your brother did. He landed last week from Ireland with a wooden leg, and said he, 'Where shall I come to the speech of one Steadfast Kenton? I have a greeting from his brother, the peculiarly favoured,' or some such word, 'Jephthah Kenton, who told me I should hear tidings of him from Mrs. Bakester Lightfoot, at the sign of the "Wheatsheaf."' I told him where you abode, and he said he knew as much from your brother, but he could not be tramping out to Elmwood on a wooden leg. So says I 'I will send Steadfast Kenton to you next market day.' You will find him at the sign at the 'Golden Bridle,' by the Wharf Stairs."

Stead had no sooner disposed of his wares than he went in search of the loriner's shop, really one for horse furniture. There was a bench outside, looking out on the wharf and shipping, and on it was seated the returned soldier, with a little party round him, to whom he was expounding what sounded more military than religious:

"And so, the fort having been summoned and quarter promised, if so be no resistance were made, always excepting Popish priests, and—Eh! What now? Be you an old neighbour? I don't remember your face."

"I have seen you, though. I am Jephthah Kenton's brother, that you asked for."

"I mind you were but a stripling in those days, and yet in gross darkness. Yea, I have a letter for thee from my comrade, who is come to high preferment."

"Jeph!"

"Yea, things have prospered with him. He was a serjeant even before we sailed for Ireland, and there he did such good service in hunting out Popish priests and rebels in their lurking places in the bogs and mountains, that the Lord General hath granted him the land that he took with his sword and his bow, even a meadow land fat and fertile, Ballyshea by name, full of the bulls of Bashan, goodly to look at. And to make all sure, he hath taken to wife the daughter of the former owner of the land a damsel fair to look upon."

"Jeph! But sure—the Irish are Papists."

"Not the whole of them. There are those that hold to Prelacy and call themselves King's men, following the bloody and blinded Duke of Ormond. Of them was this maid's father, whom we slew at the taking of Clonmel, where I got this wound and left my good right leg. So is the race not to the swift, nor the battle to the strong, but time and chance happeneth to all. When I could hobble about once more on crutches, I found that the call had come to divide and possess the gate of the enemy, and that the meads of Ballyshea had fallen to Serjeant Kenton. Moreover, in the castle hard by, dwelt the widow and her daughter, who cried to General Lambert for their land, and what doth he say to Jephthah, but 'Make it sure, Kenton. Take the maid to wife, and so none will disturb you in the fair heritage.' Yea, and mine old comrade would have me sojourn with him till I was quite restored, so far as a man with one limb short may be. I tell you 'tis a castle, man."

"Our Jeph lord of a castle?"

"Aye, even so. Twice as big as Elmwood Hall, if half were not in ruins, and the other half the rats run over like peas out of a bag. While as to the servants, there are dozens of them, mostly barefoot and in rags, who will run at the least beck from the old mistress or the young mistress, though they scowl at the master. But he is taking order with them, and teaching them who is to be obeyed."

"Then our Jephthah is a great man?"

"You may say that—a bigger man than the squire at Elmwood, or at Leigh I can tell you. Only I would give all that bare mountain and bog, full of wild, Popish, red-haired kernes for twenty yards in a tidy street at Bristol, with decent godly folk around me. Murdering or being murdered, I have marvelled more than once whether the men of Israel were as sick of it in Canaan as I was at Drogheda, but the cry ever was, 'Be not slack in the work.' But I will bring you Jephthah's letter. He could not write when he went off, but he could not be a serjeant without, so we taught him—I and Corporal Faith-Wins."

Jephthah's handwriting was of a bold description doing honour to his tutors, but the letter was very brief, though to the purpose—

"Dear Brothers and Sisters,

"This is to do you, to wit, that by the grace of Heaven on my poor endeavours I am come to high preferment. A goodly spoil hath fallen unto me, namely, the castle and lands of Ballyshea, and therewith the daughter of the owner, deceased, by name Ellen Roche, whom I have espoused in marriage, and am bringing to the light of truth. I have castle, lands, flocks and herds, men-servants and maid-servants in abundance, and I give thanks to Him who hath rewarded His servant.

"Therefore I wholly resign to you, my brethren, Steadfast and Benoni, any rights of heirship that may be mine in respect of the farmstead of Elmwood, and will never, neither I nor my heirs, trouble you about it further. Yet if Ben, or my sisters Patience and Jerusha, be willing to cross over to me in this land of promise they shall be kindly welcome, and I shall find how to bestow them well in marriage. Mine old comrade, Seth Coleman, will tell them how to reach the Castle of Ballyshea, and how to find safe convoy, and tell you more of the estate wherewith it has pleased Heaven to reward my poor services.

"And so commending you to His holy keeping, no more from your loving brother,

"JEPHTHAH KENTON."

The spelling of this was queer, even according to the ways of the time, but it was not hard to understand, and it might well fill Steadfast with amazement.

He longed to share the tidings with Emlyn, but he did not feel as if it would be right to let anyone hear before Patience. Only as he went back and called again at Mrs. Lightfoot's for his basket, she asked whether he had found Seth Coleman, and if his brother had come to such preferment as was reported.

"Yea," said Steadfast, "he hath a grant of land, and a castle, and a wife."

"Eh, now! Lack-a-day! 'Tis alway the most feather-pated that fly highest."

Cromwell's Ironsides feather-pated! But that did not trouble Steadfast, who all the way home, as he rode his donkey, was thinking of the difference it made in his prospects, and in what he had to offer Emlyn to be able to feel his tenure so much more secure.

Patience and Ben listened in utter amazement ending in a not complimentary laugh on the part of the former. "Our Jeph lord of a castle? I'd like to see him."

"Would you? He has a welcome and a husband ready for you and Rusha both?"

"D'ye think I would go and leave you for Jeph, if he were lord of ten castles?"

And Ben, whose recollections of Jeph were very dim, exclaimed, "Lord of a castle! I shall have a crow over Nick Blane now!"

Rusha, who was well content with her service at the hall, had no mind for such a terrible enterprise as a journey "beyond seas" to Ireland, and mayhap Jeph's prospective husband was a less tempting idea, because a certain young groom had shown symptoms of making her his sweetheart.

Steadfast thought often of telling the great secret of his heart to his faithful sister Patience, but his extreme shyness and modesty, and the reserve in which he always lived, seemed to make it impossible to him to broach the subject, and there might be a certain consciousness that Emlyn, while his own pet, had been very troublesome to Patience.

Stead was two-and-twenty, a sturdy well-grown fellow, but the hard work he had been obliged to do as a growing lad, had rounded his shoulders, and he certainly did not walk like the men who had been drilled for soldiers. His face was healthy and sunburnt, with fair short hair and straightforward grey eyes. At the first glance people would say, "What a heavy-looking, clownish young man," but at the second there was something that made a crying child in the street turn to him for help in distress, and made the marketing dames secure that he told the truth about his wares.

Patience was rather startled by seeing him laboriously tying up a posy of wild rose, honeysuckle, and forget-me-not, and told him the Bristol folks would not buy those common wild flowers.

"They are for none of them," replied Stead, a little gruffly, and colouring hotly at being caught.

"Oh!" said Patience, in her simplicity. "Are they for Emlyn? I do not think her mistress will let you see her."

"I shall," said Stead. "She ought to know of our good fortune."

"He has forgotten that Emlyn is not our sister after all," said Patience, as she went back to her washing.

"She might as well," said Ben, who could not remember the hut without Emlyn.

Stead had better luck than Patience foreboded from a household where the servants were kept very strictly, for there was a good deal of curiosity in Bristol about the report that a lad from the neighbourhood had won an Irish heiress and castle, and when Stead presented himself at the door of the house under the overhanging gable, and begged to see Emlyn Gaythorn to give her some tidings, the maid who opened it exclaimed, "Is it anent the castle in Ireland?"

Stead awkwardly said "Aye, mistress." And as it became evident that the readiest way of learning the facts would be his admission, he was let into the house into a sort of wainscotted hall, where he found the mistress herself superintending three or four young sempstresses who were making shirts for the gentlemen of the garrison. Emlyn was among them, and sprang up looking as if white seams were not half so congenial as nutting in the gulley, but she looked prettier than ever, as the little dark curls burst out of the prim white cap, she sniffed the flowers with ecstasy, and her eyes danced with delight that did Stead's heart good to see. He needed it, for to stand there hat in hand before so many women all staring at him filled him with utter confusion, so that he could scarcely see, and stumbled along when Mrs. Sloggett called, "Come here, young man. Is it true that it is your brother who has won a castle and a countess in Ireland?"

"Not a countess, ma'am," said Stead, gruff with shyness, "but a castle."

Mrs. Sloggett put him through a perfect catechism on Jeph and his fortunes, which he answered at first almost monosyllabically, though afterwards he could speak a little more freely, when the questions did not go quite beyond his knowledge. Finally he succeeded in asking permission to take Emlyn and show her his brother's letter. Mrs. Sloggett was gracious to the brother of the lord of a castle, even in Ireland, and moreover Emlyn was viewed in the light of one of the Kenton family.

So leave was granted to take Master Kenton (he had never been so called before) out into the garden of pot-herbs behind the house, and Emlyn with her dancing step led the way, by a back door down a few steps into a space where a paved walk led between two beds of vegetables, bordered with a narrow edge of pinks, daisies, and gilliflowers, to a seat under the shade of an old apple tree, looking out, as this was high ground, over the broad river full of shipping.

"Stead! Stead, good old Stead," she cried, "to come just as I was half dead with white seam and scolding! Emlyn here! Emlyn there! And she's ready with her fingers too. She boxed mine ears till they sang again yesterday."

"The jade," muttered Stead. "What for?"

"Only for looking out at window," said Emlyn. "How could I help it, when there were six outlandish sailors coming up the street leading a big black bear. Well, Stead, and are you all going to live with Jeph in his castle, and will you take me?"

"He asks me not," said Stead, and began to read the letter, to which Emlyn listened with many little remarks. "So Patience and Rusha wont go. I marvel at them, yet 'tis like sober-sided old Patty! And mayhap among the bogs and hills 'tis lonelier than in the gulley. I mind a trooper who had served in Ireland telling my father it was so desolate he would not banish a dog there. But what did he say about home, Stead, I thought it was all yours?"

Stead explained, and also the possibility of endeavouring to rebuild the farmhouse. If he could go to Mr. Elmwood with thirty pounds he thought it might be done. "And then, Emlyn, when that is saved (and I have five pounds already), will you come and make it your home for good and all?"

"Stead! oh Stead! You don't mean it—you—Why, that's sweethearting!"

"Well, so it is, Emlyn," said Stead, a certain dignity taking the place of his shyness now it had come to the point. "I ask you to be my little sweetheart now, and my wife when I have enough to make our old house such as it was when my good mother was alive."

"Stead, Stead, you always were good to me! Will it take long, think you? I would save too, but I have but three crowns the year, and that sour-faced Rachel takes all the fees."

"The thing is in the hands of God. It must depend on the crops, but with this hope before me, I will work as never man worked before," said Stead.

"And I will be mistress there!" cried Emlyn.

"My wife will be mistress wherever I am sweet."

"Ah, ha!" she laughed, "now I have something to look to, I shall heed little when the dame flouts me and scolds me, and Joan twits me with her cousin the 'prentice."

They had only just time to go through the ceremony of breaking a tester between them before a shrill call of "Emlyn" resounded down the garden. Mrs. Sloggett thought quite time enough had been wasted over the young man, and summoned the girl back to her sewing.

Emlyn made a face of disgust, very comical and very joyous, but as the good dame was actually coming in search of her no more could pass.

Stead went away overflowing with happiness, and full of plans of raising the means of bringing back this sunshine of his hearth. Perhaps it was well that, though slow of thought, Patience still had wit enough in the long hours of the day to guess that the nosegay boded something. She could not daunt or damp Steadfast's joy—nay, she had affection enough for the pretty little being she had cherished for seven years to think she shared it—but she knew all the time that there would be no place in that new farmhouse for her, and there was a chill over her faithful heart at times. But what would that signify, she thought, provided that Stead was happy?

CHAPTER XIX

PATIENCE

"I'm the wealthy miller yet."
TENNYSON.

Most devoted was the diligence with which Steadfast toiled and saved with the hope before him. Since the two young girls were no longer at home, and Ben had grown into a strong lad, Stead held that many little indulgences might be dispensed with, one by one, either because they cost money or prevented it from being acquired. No cheese was bought now, and he wanted to sell all the butter and all the apples that were not defective.

Patience contrived that Ben should never be stinted of his usual fare; and she would, not allow that he needed no warm coat for the winter, but she said nothing about the threadbare state of her own petticoat, and she stirred nothing but the thinnest buttermilk into her own porridge, and not even that when the little pigs required it. It was all for Stead.

Patience at twenty was not an uncomely maiden so far as kindly blue eyes, fresh healthy cheeks, and perfect neatness could make her agreeable to look at, but there was an air of carefulness, and of having done a great deal of hard work, which had made her seem out of the reach of the young men who loitered and talked with the maidens on the village green, and looked wistfully at the spot where the maypole had once stood.

Patience was the more amazed by a visit from the Miller Luck and his son. The son was a fine looking young man of three or four and twenty, who had about three years before married a farmer's daughter, and had lost her at the birth of her second child. There he stood, almost as bashful as Stead himself could have been under the circumstances, while his father paid the astonished Patience the compliment of declaring that they had put their heads together, and made up their minds that there was no wench in those parts so like to be a good mother to the babes, nor so thrifty a housewife as she; and, that, though there were plenty of maids to be had who could bring something in their hands, her ways were better than any portion she could bring.

It really was a splendid offer. The position of miller's wife was very prosperous, and the Lucks were highly respected. The old miller was good and kindly, Andrew Luck the steadiest of young men, and though not seen to much advantage as he stood sheepishly moving from leg to leg, he was a very fine, tall, handsome youth, with a certain sweetness and wistfulness in his countenance. Patience had no scruples about previous love and courtship. That was not the point as she answered—

"Thank you, Master Luck, you are very good; but I cannot leave my brothers."

"Let the big one get a wife of his own then," and, as Patience shook her head, and glanced at where Ben, shy of strangers, was cutting rushes, "and if you be tender on the young one, there would be work for him about the place. I know you have been a good mother to him, you'd be the same to our little ones. Come, Andrew, can't ye say a word for yourself?"

"Come, Patience, do 'ee come!" pleaded poor Andrew, and the tears even sprang to his eyes. "I'd be very good to thee, and I know thou would'st be to my poor babes."

Patience's heart really warmed to him, and still more to the babes, but she could only hold out.

"You must find another," she said.

"Come, you need not be coy, my lass," said the old miller. "You'll not get a better offer, and Andrew has no time nor heart either for running about courting. What he wants is a good wife to cheer him up, and see to the poor little children."

It was powerful pleading, and Patience felt it.

"Aye, Master Miller," she said, "but you see I'm bound not to leave Steadfast till he is married. He could not get on no ways without me."

"Then why—a plague on it—don't he wed and have done with it?"

"He cannot," said Patience, "till he has made up enough to build up our old house, but that won't be yet awhile—for years maybe; and he could not do it without me to help him."

"And what's to become of you when you've let your best years go by a-toiling for him, and your chance is gone by, and his wife turns you to the door?" said Master Luck, not very delicately.

"That God will provide," said Patience, reverently. "Anyway, I must cleave to Steadfast though 'tis very good of you, Master Luck and Master Andrew, and I never could have thought of such a thing, and I am right sorry for the little ones."

"If you would only come and see them!" burst out the poor young father. "You never see such a winsome little poppet as Bess. And they be so young now, they'd never know you were not their own mother."

"Don't, don't, Master Andrew!" cried Patience, "I tell you I'd come if I could, but you can't wait, and they can't wait; and you must find a good mother at once for them, for I have passed my word to hold by Stead till he is married, and I must keep to it."

"Very well, my lass," said the miller, grimly. "There's wenches better portioned and better favoured than you, and I hope you won't have to repent of missing a good offer."

Of course he said it as if he hoped she would. Patience cried heartily when they were gone. Ben came up to her and glowered after them, declaring he wouldn't have his Patty go to be only a step-mother to troublesome brats; but Stead, when he came to know of it, looked grave, and said it was very good of Pat; but he wished she could have kept the young fellow in play till she was ready for him.

Goody Grace, who was looking after the children till the stepmother could be found, came and expostulated with Patience, telling her she was foolish to miss such a chance, and that she would find out her mistake when Stead married and that little flighty, light-headed wench made the place too hot to hold her. What would she do then?

"Come and help you nurse the folk, Goody," said Patience, cheerfully.

Her heart would fail her sometimes at the outlook, but she was too busy to think much about it. Only the long evenings had been pleasanter when Stead used to teach Ben to read Dr. Eales's books and tell her bits such as she could understand than now when he grudged a candle big enough to be of any use, and was only plaiting rushes and reckoning up what everything would bring.

Ben was a bright little fellow, and could read as well as his brother. He longed for school, for when boys were not obliged to learn, some of them wished to do so. There was a free grammar school about three miles off to which he wanted to go, and Patience, who was proud of his ability, wished to send him, neither of them thinking anything of the walk.

Stead, however, could see no use in more learning than he had himself. Neither he nor Jeph had been to school. Why should the child go? He could not be spared just as he was getting old enough to be of some use and save time, which was money.

And when the little fellow showed his disappointment, Stead was even surly in telling him "they wanted no upstarts."

It was a hard winter, and the frost was followed by a great deal of wet. One of the sheep was swept away by the flood; three or four lambs died; and Stead, for about the first time in his life, caught a severe feverish cold in looking after the flock, and was laid by for a day or two, very cross and fretful at everything going wrong without him.

Poor little Ben was more railed at for those few days than ever he had been before, and next he broke down and had to be nursed; and then came Patience's turn. She was ill enough to frighten her brothers; and Goody Grace, who came to see to her, finding how thin her blanket was, and how long it was since she had had any food but porridge, gave Steadfast a thorough good scolding, told him he would be the death of a better sister than he deserved, and set before him how only for his sake Patience might be living on the fat of the land at the mill.

To all appearance, Stead listened sulkily enough, but by-and-by Goody found a fowl killed and laid ready for use. It was an old hen, whose death set Patience crying in her weakness. Nevertheless, it was stewed down into broth which heartened her up considerably, and a blanket that came home rolled up on the donkey's back warmed her heart as much as her limbs.

Mrs. Elmwood spared Rusha for a week, and it was funny to see how the girl wondered at its having been possible to live in such a den. She absolutely cried when Ben told her how hard they had been living, and said she did not think Stead would ever have used Patience so.

"Then why did she make as if she liked it?" said Stead, gruffly.

But for all that Stead was too sound-hearted not to be grieved at himself, and to see that his love and impatience had led him into unkindness to those who depended on him; and when Master Woodley preached against love of money he felt pricked at the heart, though it had not been the gain in itself that he aimed at. And when he had to go to the mill, the sight of the comfortable great kitchen, with the open hearth, glowing fire, seats on either side, tall settle, and the flitches of bacon on the rafters, seemed to reproach him additionally. The difficulties there had been staved off by the old miller himself marrying a stout, motherly widow, who had a real delight in the charge of a baby.

"For," said Master Luck, "Andrew and I could agree on no one for him."

Moreover, Stead ceased to grunt contemptuously when Patience, with Goody Grace to back her, declared that Ben was too young and slight for farm work.

The boy was allowed to trudge his daily three miles to school, and there his progress was the wonder and delight of his slower-witted brother and sister.

CHAPTER XX

EMLYN'S SERVICE

"Oh, blind mine eye that would not trace,
And deaf mine ear that would not heed
The mocking smile upon her face,
The mocking voice of greed."
                    LEWIS CARROLL.

When Lady-day came round, Steadfast found to his delight and surprise a little figure dancing out to meet him from Mrs. Lightfoot's.

"There, Master Stead. Are not you glad to see me, or be you too dumbfounded to get out a word, like good old Jenny?" stroking the donkey's ears. "Posies of primroses! How sweet they be! You must spare me one."

"As many as you will, sweetheart. They be all for you, whether given or sold. And you've got a holiday for Lady-day."

"Have a care! I got my ears boxed for such a Popish word. 'Tis but quarter day, you know, being that, hang, draw, and quarter is more to the present folks' mind than ladies or saints. I have changed my service, you must know, as poor Dick used to sing:—

"Have a new master, be a new man."

"You have not heard from your own folk," cried Stead, this being what he most dreaded.

"Nay. But I can away no more with Dame Sloggett, and Cross-patch Rachel, white seam and salmon, and plain collars. So I bade her farewell at the end of the year, and I've got a new mistress."

Stead stood with open mouth. To change service at the end of a year was barely creditable in those days, and to do so without consultation with home was unkind and alarming.

"There now, don't be crooked about it. I had not time to come out and tell you and Patience, the old crones kept me so close, stitching at shirts for a captain that is to sail next week, and I knew you would be coming in."

"Where is it?" was all Stead uttered.

"What think you of Master Henshaw's, the great merchant, and an honest well-wisher to King and Church to boot?"

"Master Henshaw, the West Indian merchant? His is a good, well-ordered household, and he holds with the old ways."

"Yes. He was out that Whitsun morning we wot of," said Emlyn. "I wist well you would be pleased."

"But I thought his good lady was dead," said Steadfast.

"So she is. She that came out to the gully, but there's a new Mistress Henshaw, a sweet young lady, of a loyal house, the Ayliffes of Calfield. And I am to be her own woman."

"Own woman," said Mrs. Lightfoot, for they were by this time among the loaves in her stall. "Merchants' wives did not use to have women of their own in my time."

For this was the title of a lady's maid, and rules as to household appointments were strictly observed before the rebellion.

"Mistress Henshaw is gentlewoman born," returned Emlyn, with a toss of her head. "She ought to have all that is becoming her station in return for being wedded to an old hunks like that! And 'tis very well she should have one like *me* who has seen what becomes good blood! So commend me to Patience and Rusha, and tell Ben maybe I shall have an orange to send him one of these days. And cheer up, Stead. I shall get five crowns and two gowns a year, and many a fee besides when there is company, so we may build the house the sooner, and I shall not be mewed up, and shall see the more of thee. 'Tis all for you. So never look so gloomy on it, old Sobersides."

And she turned her sweet face to him, and coaxed and charmed him into being satisfied that all was well, dwelling on the loyalty and excellence of the master of the house.

He found it true that it was much easier to see Emlyn than before. Mrs. Henshaw, a pretty young creature, not much older than Emlyn, was pleased to do her own marketing, and came out attended by Emlyn, and a little black slave boy carrying a basket. She generally bought all that Steadfast had to sell, and then gave smiling thanks when he offered to help carry home her purchases. She would join company with some of her acquaintance, and leave the lovers to walk together, only accompanied by little Diego, or Diggo as they called him, whose English was of the most rudimentary description.

Emlyn certainly was very happy in her new quarters. Neither her lady nor herself was arrayed with the rigid plainness exacted by Puritanism, and many disapproving glances were cast upon the fair young pair, mistress and maid, by the sterner matrons. Waiting women could not indulge in much finery, but whatever breast knots and tiny curls beyond her little tight cap could do, Emlyn did without fear of rebuke. Stead tried to believe that the disapproving looks and words, by which Mrs. Lightfoot intimated that she heard reports unfavourable to the household were only due to the general distrust and dislike to the bright and lively Emlyn. Mrs. Lightfoot was no Puritan herself, but her gossips were, and he received her observations with a dull, stony look that vexed her, by intimating that it was no business of hers.

Still it was borne in upon him that, good man as Mr. Henshaw certainly was, the household was altered. It had been poverty and distress which had led the Ayliffe family to give their young sister to a man so much her elder, and inferior in position; and perhaps still more a desire to confirm the Royalist footing in the city of Bristol. The lady's brothers were penniless Cavaliers, and one of them made her house his home, and a centre of Royalist plots and intelligences, which excited Emlyn very much by the certainty that something was going on, though what it was, of course, she did not know; and at any rate there was coming and going, and all sorts of people were to be seen at the merchant's hospitable table, all manner of news to be had here, there, and everywhere, with which she delighted to entertain Steadfast, and show her own importance.

It was not often good news as regarded the Cavalier cause, for Cromwell was fixing himself in his seat; and every endeavour to hatch a scheme against him was frustrated, and led to the flight or death of those concerned in it. However, so long as Emlyn had something to tell, it made little difference whether the tidings were good or bad, whether they concerned Admiral Blake's fleet, or her mistress's little Italian greyhound. By-and-by however instead of Mrs. Henshaw, there came to market Madam Ayliffe, her mother, a staid, elderly lady, all in black, who might as well, Emlyn said, have been a Puritan.

She looked gravely at Stead, and said, "Young man, I am told that you are well approved and trustworthy, and that my daughter suffers you to walk home with this maiden, you being troth plight to her."

Stead assented.

"I will therefore not forbid it, trusting that if you be, as I hear, a prudent youth, you may bring her to a more discreet and obedient behaviour than hath been hers of late."

So saying, Mrs. Ayliffe joined company with the old Cavalier Colonel and went on her way as Emlyn made that ugly face that Stead knew of old, clenched her hand and muttered, "Old witch! She is a Puritan at heart, after all! She is turning the house upside down, and my poor mistress has not spirit to say 'tis her own, with the old woman and the old hunks both against her! Why, she threatened to beat me because, forsooth, the major's man was but giving me the time of day on the stairs!"

"Was that what she meant?" asked Stead.

"Assuredly it was. Trying to set you against me, the spiteful old make-bate, and no one knows how long she will be here, falling on the poor lads if they do but sing a song in the hall after supper, as if she were a very Muggletonian herself. I trow she is no better."

"Did you not tell me how she held out her house against the Roundheads, and went to prison for sheltering Cavaliers?"

"I only wish they had kept her there. All old women be Puritans at heart. I say Stead, I'll have done with service. Let us be wed at once."

Stead could hardly breathe at this proposition. "But I have only nine pounds and two crowns and—" he began.

"No matter, there be other ways," she went on. "Get the house built, and I'll come, and we will have curds and whey all the summer, and mistress and all her friends will come out and drink it, and eat strawberries!"

"But the Squire will never build the place up unless I bring more in hand."

"You 'but' enough to butt down a wall, you dull-pated old Stead," said Emlyn, "you know where to get at more, and so do I."

Stead's grey eyes fixed on her in astonishment and bewilderment.

"Numskull!" she exclaimed, but still in that good humoured voice of banter that he never had withstood, "you know what I mean, though maybe you would not have me say it in the street, you that have secrets."

"How do you know of it?"

"Have not I eyes, though some folk have not? Could not I look out at a chink on a fine summer morning, when you thought the children asleep? Could not I climb up to your precious cave as well as yourself; and hear the iron clink under the stone. Ha, ha! and you and Patience thought no one knew but yourselves."

"I trust no one else does."

"No, no, I'm no gad-about, whatever you may be pleased to think me. They say everything comes of use in seven years, and it must be over that now."

"Ten since 'twas hidden, nigh seven since that Whitsuntide. There's never a parson who could come out, is there? Besides, with Peter Woodward nigh, 'tis not safe to meet."

"That's what your head is running on. No, no. They will never have it out again that fashion. The old Prayer-book is banished for ever and a day! I heard master and the Captain say that now old Noll has got his will, he will soon call himself king, and there's no hope of churches or parsons coming back; and old madam sat and cried. The Jack Presbyters and the rest of the sectaries have got it all their own way."

"Dr. Eales said I had no right to give it to Master Woodley, or any that was not the right sort."

"So why should you go on keeping it there rotting for nothing, when it might just hinder us from wearing our very lives out while you are plodding and saving?"

Stead stood stock still, as her meaning dawned on him, "Child, you know not what you say," at last he uttered.

"Ah well, you are slow to take things in; but you'll do it at last."

"I am slow to take in this," said Stead. "Would you have me rob God?"

"No, only the owls and the bats," said Emlyn. "If they are the better for the silver and gold under them! What good can it do to let it lie there and rot?"

"Gold rots not!" growled Stead.

"Tarnishes, spoils then!" said Emlyn pettishly. "Come, what good is't to any mortal soul there?"

"It is none of mine."

"Not after seven years? Come, look you now, Stead, 'tis not only being tired of service and sharp words, and nips and blows, but I don't like being mocked for having a clown and a lubber for my sweetheart. Oh yes! they do, and there's a skipper and two mates, and a clerk, and a well-to-do locksmith, besides gentlemen's valets and others, I don't account of, who would all cut off their little fingers if I'd only once look at them as I am doing at you, you old block, who don't heed it, and I don't know that I can hold out against them all," she added, looking down with a sudden shyness; "specially the mates. There's Jonah Richards, who has a ship building that he is to have of his own, and he wants to call it the 'Sprightly Emlyn,' and the other sailed with Prince Rupert, and made ever so many prizes, and how am I to stand out when you don't value me the worth of an old silver cup?"

"Come, come, Em, that's only to frighten a man." But she knew in his tone that he was frightened.

"Not a bit! I should be ever so much better off in a tidy little house where I could see all that came and went than up in your lane with nought to go by but the market folk. 'Tis not everyone that would have kept true to a big country lout like you, like that lady among the salvage men that the King spoke of; and I get nothing by it but wait, wait, wait, when there's stores of silver ready to your hand."

"Heaven knows, and you know, Emlyn, 'tis not for want of love."

"Heaven may know, but I don't."

"I gave my solemn word."

"And you have kept it these ten years, and all is changed." Then altering her tone, "There now, I know it takes an hour to beat a notion into that slow brain of yours, and here we be at home, and I shall have madam after me. I'll leave you to see the sense of it, and if I do not hear of something before long, why then I shall know how much you care for poor little Emlyn."

With which last words she flitted within the gates, leaving Steadfast still too much stunned to realise all she meant, as he turned homewards; but all grew on him in time, the idea that Emlyn, his Emlyn, his orphan of the battlefield, bereaved for the sake of King and Church, should be striving to make him betray his trust! "The silver is Mine and the gold is Mine," rang in his ears, and yet was it not cruel that when she really loved him best, and sought to return to him as a refuge from the many temptations to her lively spirit, he should be forced to leave her in the midst of them—against her own warning and even entreaty, and not only himself lose her, but lose her to one of those godless riotous sailors who were the dread and bane of the neighbourhood? Was not a human soul worth as much as a consecrated Chalice?

These were the debates in Steadfast's much tormented soul. He could think, though he could not clothe his thoughts in words, and day after day, night after night he did think, while Patience wondered at the heavy moodiness that seemed to have come over him. He would not open his lips to ask her counsel, being quite certain of what it would be, and not choosing to hear her censure of Emlyn for what he managed to excuse by the poor child's ignorance and want of training, and by her ardent desire to be under his wing and escape from temptation.

He recollected a thousand pleas that he might have used with her, to show it was not want of love but a sacred pledge that withheld him, and market day after market day he went in, priming himself all the way with arguments that were to confirm her constancy, arm her against temptation, and assure her of his unalterable love, though he might not break his vow, nor lay his hand upon sacred things.

But whether Emlyn would not, or could not, meet him, he did not know, for a week or two went by before he saw her, and then she was carrying a great fan for her young mistress, who was walking with a Cavalier, as gay as Cavaliers ever ventured to be, and another young lady, whose waiting woman had paired with Emlyn. They were mincing along, gazing about them, and uttering little contemptuous titters, and Stead could only too well guess what kind of remarks Emlyn's companion might make upon him.

Near his stand, however, the other lady beckoned her maid to adjust something in her dress; and Stead could approach Emlyn. She looked up with her bright, laughing eyes with a certain wistfulness in them.

"Have you made up your mind to cheat the owls?" she asked.

"Emlyn, if you would not speak so lightly, I could show cause—"

"Oh, that's enough," she answered hastily, turning as the other maid joined her; and Stead caught the shrill, pert voice demanding if that was her swain with clouted shoes. Emlyn's reply he could not hear, but he saw the twist of the shoulders.

There are bitter moments in everyone's life, and that was one of the very bitterest of Steadfast Kenton's.

CHAPTER XXI

THE ASSAULT OF THE CAVERN

"By all description this should be the place.
Who's here?"
SHAKESPEARE.

Harvest was over, and the autumn evenings were darkening. It was later than the usual bed time, but Patience had a piece of spinning which she was anxious to finish for the weaver who took all her yarn, and Stead was reading Dr. Eales's gift of the Morte d'Arthur, which had great fascination for him, though he never knew whether to regard it as truth or fable. He wanted to drive out the memory of what Mrs. Lightfoot had told him about the Henshaw household, where the youngest of the lady's brothers had lately arrived from beyond seas, bringing with him habits of noise and riot, which greatly scandalised the neighbours.

Suddenly Growler started up with pricked ears, and emitted a sound like thunder. Patience checked her wheel. There was an unmistakable sound of steps. Stead sprang up. Growler rushed at the door with a furious volley of barking. Stead threw it open, catching up a stout stick as he did so, and the dog dashed out, but was instantly driven back with an oath and a blow. It was a bright moonlight night, and Stead beheld three tall men evidently well armed.

"Ho, you fellow there," one called out, "keep back your cur, we don't want to hurt him nor you."

"Then what are you doing here?" demanded Stead.

"We are come for what you wot of. For the King's service."

"Who sent you?" asked Stead, for the moment somewhat dazed.

One of them laughed and said, "As if you did not know."

There was a sickening perception, but Stead's powers were alert enough for him to exclaim, "Then you have no warrant."

"My good fellow, don't stickle about such trifles. For the King's service it is, and that should be enough for all loyal hearts. Hollo, what's that? Silence your dog, I say," as Growler's voice resounded through the gulley, "or it will be the worse for you and him."

Stead took hold of the dog's collar, and amidst his choked grumbles, said, "I do nought but on true warrant."

"Hark ye, blockhead," said the foremost. "I'm an officer of His Majesty's, with power to make requisitions for his service."

"Shew it," said Stead, quite convinced that this was sheer robbery.

"You addle-pated, insolent clown, to dispute terms with gentlemen in His Majesty's service. Stand aside. I've done you only too much honour by parleying with you. Out of the way. We don't want to take a stick of your own trumpery, I say."

"Sir, it is Church plate."

"Ha, ha! Church plate is His Most Sacred Majesty's plate. Don't ye know that, you ass? Here! we'll throw you back something for yourself if you will show us the cave and save us trouble, for we know which it is by the token of the red stone and twisted ash. Ho! take—What's become of the clown? He has run off. Discreet fellow!"

For Stead had disappeared in the black darkness behind the hut. He remembered Jephthah's discomfiture by the owl, and it struck him that from within the cavern it would be quite possible to keep the robbers at bay, if they tried without knowing the way to climb up among the bushes. He was not afraid for his brother and sister, as the marauders evidently did not want anything but the plate. Indeed, his whole soul was so concentrated on the defence of his charge that he had no room for anything else.

Knowing the place perfectly, Stead had time to swing himself, armed with a stout bludgeon, up into the hermit's cave, and even to drag after him Growler, a very efficient ally. The contrasts of moonlight were all in his favour, the lights almost as bright as in sunshine, the shadows so very dark. He could see through the overhanging ivy and travellers' joy the men peering about with their dark lantern, looking into the caves where the pigs were, among the trees, and he held Growler's mouth together lest the grim murmurs that were rolling in the beast's throat should serve as a guide.

Then he heard them shout to Patience to come and guide them since her coward of a brother had made off, and he heard her answer, "Not I, 'tis no business of mine."

"We'll see about that. D'ye know how folks are made to speak, my lass?"

Then Stead recollected with horror that he had left her to her fate. Would he be obliged to come down to her help? At that moment, however, there was a call from the fellow who bore the lantern. "Here's the red stone. That must be the ash. Now then!"

"You first, Nick." Then came a crackling and rustling of boughs, a head appeared, and at that moment Stead loosed Growler and would have dealt a blow with his stick, but that the assault of the dog had sufficed to send the assailant, roaring and cursing, headlong down the crag.

Furious threats came up to him and his dog, but he heard them in silence, though Growler's replies were vociferous. Stead gathered that the fall had in some degree hurt the man for he made an exclamation of pain, and the others bade him stay there and keep back the wench.

"We'll have you down though we smoke you out like a wasps' nest, you disloyal adder, you," was one of the threats.

"Or serve him like the Spaniard at Porto Santo," said another.

Presently after numerous threats and warnings that they had firearms and were determined to use them, two of the men began climbing much more cautiously, holding by the trees, so as not to be suddenly overthrown. However the furious attack of such a dog as Growler, springing from utter darkness was a formidable matter, and the man against whom he had launched himself could not but fall in his turn, but the dog went after him, and the companion, being on his guard, was not overthrown. Stead aimed a blow at the fellow with all his might, but the slouching hat warded off the full force of the bludgeon. Then Stead sprang at him and grappled with him. There was the report of a pistol, and both rolled headlong among the bushes, but at that moment a fresh shout was heard—a cry of "Villains, traitors, robbers—what be at?" and a rush of feet, while in the moonlight appeared Peter Pierce with his fowling piece, another man, Ben, and four or five dogs.

The robbers never waited to see how small the reinforcement was, and it made noise enough for the whole hue-and-cry of the parish. Off they dashed, through the wood, the new comers after them.

But all Patience knew was that Steadfast was lying senseless at the bottom of the cliff, with poor Growler moaning by him, and licking his face, and that her hands were wet with what must be blood.

It was too dark to see anything, but she could hardly bear to leave him, as she hurried back to the hut for the lantern. All this had taken but few minutes, so that she had only to catch it up from the table where Stead's book still lay.

By the time she came back, he had opened his eyes, and his hand was on Growler's head.

"Are they gone?" he asked faintly.

"Yes, and Peter after them. Oh! Stead, you are badly hurt."

"They have not got it?"

"Oh no, no, you saved it."

"Thank God. Is Ben safe?"

"Yes, after them with Peter. I sent him out while you were talking to call Peter."

"Good—" and his eyes closed again. "Good Growler, poor Growl—" he added, fondling the big head, as the dog moaned. "See to him, Pat."

"I must see to you first. Oh! Stead, is it very bad?"

"I'll try to get in, if you'll help me."

He raised himself, but this effort brought a rush of blood to the lips, which greatly terrified Patience. To her great relief, however, Nanny Pierce having satisfied herself that all was quiet round the hut, here called out to ask where Patience was. She was profuse in "Lack-a-daisy!" "Dear heart!" and "Poor soul!" and was quite sure Stead was as good as a dead man; but she had strong arms, and so had Patience, and when they had done what they could to stanch the wound in his side, which however, was not bleeding much externally, they carried him in between them to Patience's bed which had been Emlyn's, and therefore was the least uncomfortable. Poor Growler crept after, bleeding a good deal, and Steadfast would not rest till his faithful comrade was looked to. There was a dagger cut in his chest, which Nanny, used to dog doctoring, bound up, after which the creature came close to his master, and fell asleep under his hand.

It was a very faint hand. Movement or speech alike brought blood to the mouth, and Stead's ruddy checks were becoming deadly white. He struggled to say, "You and Ben guard it! Say a prayer, Pat," and then the two women really thought that in the gush that followed all was over, and Nanny marvelled at the stunned calm in which Patience went over the Lord's Prayer, and such Psalms as she could remember.

Steps came, and Nanny shrieked. Then she saw it was her husband and the other two men.

"Made off to the town," said Peter, gruffly.

"How now—hurt?"

"O, Peter, they have made an end of the poor lad. Died like a lamb, even now."

"No, no," said Peter, as he came close to the bed with his more experienced eye; "he ain't dead. 'Tis but a swoon. Hast any strong waters, Pat? No, I'll be bound. Ho, you now, Bill, run and knock them up at the Elmwood Arms, and bring down a gill."

"And call Goody Grace," entreated Patience, "she will know best what to do."

On the whole, Peter's military experience was more hopeful, if not more helpful than Goody Grace's. He was the only person who persisted in declaring that such wounds were not always mortal, though he agreed in owning that the inward bleeding was the worst sign. Stead did not attempt to speak again, but lay there deadly white and with a stricken look on his face, which Patience could not bear to see, and she ascribed to the conviction that the wretched little Emlyn must have betrayed his secret.

The hut was over-full of volunteers of assistance and enquiry the next day, including the squire and Master Woodley; but nobody seemed to guess at the real object of the robbers' attack, everybody thinking they had come for the savings which Stead was known to be making towards rebuilding the farmhouse.

Mr. Elmwood was very indignant and took Pierce, and Blane the constable, into Bristol to see whether the felons could be captured and brought to justice, but they proved to have gone down to the wharf, and to have got on board a vessel which had dropped down the river in the early morning. They were also more than suspected of being no other than buccaneers who plied their trade of piracy in the West Indies. The younger Ayliffe had gone with them, and was by no means above suspicion.

Mr. Elmwood also brought out a barber surgeon to see young Kenton, a thing which his sister would not have dared to propose. But there was not much to be done, the doctor decided that the bullet was where the attempt at extraction would be fatal, and that the only hope of even partial recovery was in perfect stillness and silence—and this Patience could promise to ensure as far as in her lay. Instructions on dressing the wound were given to her, and she was to send in to the barber's shop if ointment or other appliances were needed. This was all that she was to expect, and more indeed than she had thought feasible; for folks of their condition were sick and got well, lived or died without the aid of practitioners above the skill of Goody Grace. However, he gave her very little hope, though he would not pronounce that her brother was dying. A few days would decide, and quiet was the only chance.

Scarcely however were the visitors gone, and Stead left to what rest pain would allow him after being handled by the surgeon, when a sound of sobbing was heard outside. "Oh! oh! I'm afraid to go in! Ben! Oh! tell me, is he not dead? I'm the most miserable maid in the world if he is."

"He's alive, small thanks to you," responded Ben, who had somehow arrived at a knowledge of the facts, while Rusha, who was milking, buried her head in Daisy's side, and would not even look at her. Patience felt in utter despair, and longed to misunderstand Stead's signs to her to open the door. She tried to impress the need of quiet, but Emlyn darted in, her hood pushed back, her hair flying, her dress disordered, looking half wild, and dropping on the floor, she crouched there with clasped hands, crying "Oh! oh! he looks like death. He'll die and I'm the most—"

"If you make all that noise and tumult he will," said Patience, who could bear no more. "Are you come here to finish what you have done? Do go away."

"Oh! but I must tell you! They said it was for the King, and that he had the right. Yes they did, and they swore that they would hurt no one."

Stead looked to a certain extent pleased, but Patience broke out, "As if you did not know he would rather die than give up his trust."

"I thought he would never know—"

"Robber!" said Patience. "Go! You have done harm enough already."

"But I must tell you," persisted Emlyn. "I used to see Dick Glass among Lord Goring's troopers, and he is from our parts, and he has been with Prince Rupert. There was a plot, I know there is, and both the Master Ayliffes are in it, and we were to go and raise Worcestershire, only they wanted money, and Dick was to—to wed me—and set us across the river this morning, when they had got the treasure. 'Twas for the King. And now they are all gone, Master Philip and all, and master says they are flibustiers, and pirates, and robbers; and Mrs. Lightfoot's boy came and said Stead Kenton was shot dead at his house door, and then I was neither to have nor to hold, but I ran off here like one distraught, for I never loved anyone like you Stead."

"Pretty love!" said Patience. "Oh! if you think you love him, go and let him be at peace."

"I do! I do!" cried the girl, quite unmanageable. "Only it made me mad that he should heed an old chest and a musty parson more than me, and so I took up with Dick, and he over persuaded me with his smooth tongue that we would raise folk for the King."

Stead held out his hand.

"Oh! Stead, Stead, you are always kinder than Patience! You forgive me, dear old Stead, do not you? And I'll tend you day and night, and you shall not die, and I'll wed you, if you have nought but the shirt to your back."

Patience felt nearly distracted at the notion of Emlyn there day and night, but at that instant Goody Grace, who had been to her home in preparation for spending the night in nursing, walked in.

"How now, mistress, what are you about here?"

"She wants to stay and tend him, and I don't know whether she has come with her mistress's knowledge," sighed Patience.

"Fine tendance!" said the old woman. "My lady wants to kill him outright. Nay, nay, my young madam, we want none of your airs and flights here. You can do no good, except by making yourself scarce—you that can't hold your tongue a moment."

Stead here whispered, "Her mistress, will she forgive her?"

"Oh, yes, no fear but that she will," said Emlyn, who perhaps had revolved in her mind, since her first impulse, what it would be to nurse Stead in that hovel, with two such displeased companions as Goody and Patience. More to pacify Steadfast's uneasy eyes than for her own sake, Patience gave her a drink of milk and a piece of bread, and Peter coming just then to ask if he could help Ben with the cattle, undertook to see her safely on her way, since twilight was coming on. Sobered and awestruck by the silence and evident condemnation of all around, she ended by flinging herself on her knees by the bed, and saying "Stead, Stead, you forgive me, though no one else does?"

"Poor child—I do—as I hope—"

"The blood again. You've done it now," exclaimed Goody Grace. "Away with you!"

Peter fairly dragged her out, while the women attended to Stead.

But he let her wait outside till they heard, "Not dead, but not far from it."

CHAPTER XXII

EMLYN'S TROTH

"Woman's love is writ in water,
Woman's faith is traced in sand."
AYTOUN.

Day after day Steadfast Kenton lingered between life and death, and though the external wound healed, there was little relief to the deeper injury which could not be reached, and which the damps and chills of autumn and winter could only aggravate.

He could move little, and speak even less; and suffered much, both from pain and difficulty of breathing, as he lay against sacks and pillows on his bed, or sat up in an elbow chair which Mrs. Elmwood lent him. Everybody was very kind in those days of danger. Mrs. Elmwood let Rusha come on many an afternoon to help her sister, and always bringing some posset, or cordial, or dainty of some sort to tempt the invalid. Goody Grace, Mrs. Blane, Dame Oates, Nanny Pierce vied with each other in offers of sitting up with him; Andrew, the young miller, came out of his way to bring a loaf of white bread, and to fetch the corn to be ground. Peter Pierce, Rusha's lover, and more old comrades than Patience quite desired, offered their services in aiding Ben with the cattle and other necessary labours, but as the first excitement wore off, these volunteers became scantier, and when nothing was to be heard but "just the same," nothing to be seen but a weak, wan figure sitting wrapped by the fire, the interest waned, and the gulley was almost as little frequented as before. Poor Ben's schooling had, of course, to be given up, and it was well that he was nearly as old as Stead had been when they were first left to themselves. Happily his fifteen months of study had not made him outgrow his filial obedience and devotion to the less instructed elder brother and sister, who had taken the place of the parents he had never known. Benoni, child of sorrow, he had been named, and perhaps his sickly babyhood and the mournful times around had tended to make him a quiet boy, without the tearing spirits that would have made him eager to join the village lads in their games. Indeed they laughed at him for his poverty and scholarship, and called him Jack Presbyter, Puritan, bookworm, and all the opprobrious names they could think of, though no one ever less merited sectarian nicknames than he, as far as doctrine went. For, bred up on Dr. Eales' books, and obliged to look out on the unsettled state of religious matters, he was as staunch a churchman as his brother, and fairly understood the foundations of his faith. Poor boy, the check to his studies disappointed him, and he spent every leisure moment over his Latin accidence or in reading. Next to the stories in the Bible, he loved the Maccabees, because of the likeness to the persecuted state of the Church; and he knew the Morte d'Arthur almost by heart, and thought it part of the history of England. Especially he loved the part that tells of the Holy Grail, the Sacred Cup that was guarded by the maimed King Pelles, and only revealed to the pure in heart and life. Stead had fully confided to him the secret of the cave, in case he should be the one left to deliver up the charge; and, in some strange way, the boy connected the treasure with the Saint Grail, and his brother with the maimed king. So he worked very hard, and Patience was capable of a good deal more than in her earlier days. Stead, helpless as he was, did not require constant attendance, and knew too well how much was on his sister's hands to trouble her when he could possibly help doing so. Thus they rubbed on; though it was a terrible winter, and they often had to break in on the hoard which was to have built the house, sometimes for needments for the patient, sometimes to hire help when there was work beyond the strength of Patience and Ben, who indeed was too slender to do all that Stead had done.

Ben did not shine in going to market. He was not big enough to hold his own against rude lads, and once came home crying with his donkey beaten and his eggs broken; moreover, he was apt to linger at stalls of books and broadsheets. As soon as Patience could venture to leave her brother, she was forced to go to market herself; and there was a staidness and sobriety about her demeanour that kept all impertinence at a distance. Poor Patience, she was not at all the laughing rustic beauty that Emlyn would have been at market. She would never have been handsome, and though she was only a few years over twenty, she was beginning to look weather-beaten and careworn, like the market women about her, mothers of half-a-dozen children.

Now and then she saw Emlyn in all her young, plump beauty, but looking much quieter, and always coming to her for news of Steadfast. There were even tears in those bright eyes when she heard how much he suffered. The girl had evidently been greatly sobered by the results of her indiscretion, and the treachery into which it had led her. She probably cared more for Steadfast than for anyone else except herself, and was shocked and grieved at his condition; and she had moreover discovered how her credulity had been played upon, and that she had had a narrow escape of being carried off by a buccaneer.

Her master too had been called to order by the authorities, fined and threatened for permitting Royalist plots to be hatched in his house. He had been angered by the younger Ayliffe's riotous doings, and his wife had been terrified. There had been a general reformation in which Emlyn had only escaped dismissal through her mistress's favour, pleading her orphanhood, her repentance, and her troth plight to the good young man who had been attacked by those dissolute fellows, though Mrs. Henshaw little knew how accountable was her favourite maid for the attack.

So good and discreet was Emlyn, so affectionate her messages to Stead, and so much brightness shone in his face on hearing them; there was so much pleasure when she sent him an orange and he returned the snowdrops he had made Rusha gather, that Patience began to believe that Stead was right—that the shock was all the maiden needed to steady her—and that all would end as he hoped, when he should be able to resume his labours, and add to the sadly reduced hoard.

It was not, however, till the March winds were over that Stead made any decided step towards recovery, and began to prefer the sun to the fire, and to move feebly and slowly about the farmyard, visiting the animals, too few in number, for his skilled attention had been missed. As summer came on he was able to do a little more, herd them with Growler's help, and gradually to undertake what required no exertion of strength or speed, and there he stopped short—all the sunny months of summer could do no more for him than make him fit to do such work as an old man of seventy might manage.

He was persuaded, much against his will, to ride the white horse into Bristol at a foot-pace to consult once more the barber surgeon. That worthy, who was unusually sagacious for his time and had had experience in the wars, told him that his recovery was a marvel, but that with the bullet where it was lodged, he could scarcely hope to enjoy much more health or comfort than at present. It could not be reached, but it might shift, when either it would prove fatal or become less troublesome; and as a friend and honest man, he counselled the poor youth not to waste his money nor torture himself by having recourse to remedies or doctors who could do no real good.

Stead thanked the barber, paid his crown, and slowly made his way to Mrs. Lightfoot's, where he was to rest, dine, and see Emlyn.

Kind Mrs. Lightfoot shed tears when she saw the sturdy, ruddy youth grown so thin and pale; and as to Emlyn, she actually stood silent for three minutes.

The two were left together in Mrs. Lightfoot's kitchen, for Patience was at market, and their hostess had to mind her trade.

Stead presently told Emlyn somewhat of the doctor's opinion, and then, producing his portion of the tester, and with lips that trembled in spite of himself, said that he had come to give Emlyn back her troth plight.

"Oh! Stead, Stead," she cried, bursting into tears. "I thought you had forgiven me."

"Forgiven you! Yea, truly, poor child, but—"

"But only when you were sick! You cast me off now you are whole."

"I shall never be whole again, Emlyn."

"I don't believe Master Willis. He is nought but a barber," she exclaimed passionately. "I know there are physicians at the Bath who would cure you; or there's the little Jew by the wharf; or the wise man on Durdham Down. But you always are so headstrong; when you have made up your mind no one can move you, and you don't care whose heart you break," she sobbed.

"Hearken, little sweet," said Stead. "'Tis nought but that I wot that it would be ill for you to be bound to a poor frail man that will never be able to keep you as you should be kept. All I had put by is well nigh gone, and I'm not like to make it up again for many a year, even if I were as strong as ever."

"And you won't go to the Jew, or the wise man, or the Bath?"

"I have not the money."

"But I will—I will save it for you!" cried Emlyn, who never had saved in her life. "Or look here. Master Henshaw might give you a place in his office, and then there would be no need to dwell in that nasty, damp gulley, but we could be in the town. I'll ask my mistress to crave it from him."

Stead could not but smile at her eagerness, but he shook his head.

"It would be bootless, sweetheart, I cannot carry weights."

"No, but you can write."

"Very scurvily, and I cannot cypher."

For Stead, like everyone else at Elmwood, kept his accounts by tally and in his head, and the mysteries of the nine Arabic figures were perfectly unknown to him. However, Emlyn stuck to the hope, and he was so far inspired by it that he ceased to insist on giving up the pledges of the betrothal, and he lay on the settle in quiet enjoyment of Emlyn's castle building, as she sat on a stool by his side, his hand on her shoulder, somewhat as it was wont to lie on Growler's head. And in spite of Master Willis's opinion, he rode home to the gulley a new man, assuring Patience, on the donkey by his side, that there was more staunchness and kindness in little Emlyn than ever they had thought for. Even the ferryman who put them over the river declared that the doctor must have done Master Kenton a power of good, and Stead smiled and did not contradict him.

Stead actually consulted Mr. Woodley how to learn cyphering beyond what Ben had acquired at school; and the minister lent him a treatise, over which he pored with a board and a burnt stick for many an hour when he was out on the common with the cattle, or on the darkening evenings in the hut. Ben saw his way into those puzzles with no more difficulty than whetted his appetite, worked out sum after sum, and explained them to his brother, to the admiration of both his elders, till frowns of despair and long sighs from Stead brought Patience to declare he was mazing himself, and insist on putting out the light.

Stead had more time for his studies than he could wish, for the cold of winter soon affected the injured lungs; and, moreover, the being no longer able to move about rapidly caused the damp and cold of the ravine to produce rheumatism and attendant ills, of which, in his former healthy, out-of-door life, he had been utterly ignorant, and he had to spend many an hour breathless, or racked with pain in the poor little hovel, sometimes trying to give his mind to the abstruse mysteries of multiplication of money, but generally in vain, and at others whiling away the time with his books, for though there were only seven of them, including Bible and Prayer-book, a very little reading could be the text of so much musing, that these few perfectly sufficed him. And then he was the nurse of any orphaned lamb or sick chicken that Patience was anxious about, and his care certainly saved many of those small lives.

The spring, when he came forth again, found him on a lower level, less strong and needing a stick to aid his rheumatic knee.

Not much was heard of Emlyn that spring. She did not come to market with her mistress, and Patience was not inclined to go in quest of her, having a secret feeling that no news might be better for Stead than anything she was likely to hear; while as to any chance of their coming together, the Kentons had barely kept themselves through this winter, and Steadfast's arithmetic was not making such progress as would give him a place at a merchant's desk.

Patience, however, was considerably startled when, one fine June day, she saw Mrs. Henshaw's servant point her out to two tall soldierly-looking men, apparently father and son.

"Good morrow to you, honest woman," said the elder. "I am told it is you who have been at charges for many years for my brother's daughter, Emlyn Gaythorn."

Patience assented.

"You have been right good to her, I hear; and I thank you for that same, and will bear what we may of the expense," he added, taking out a heavy bag from his pouch.

He went on to explain that he and his son having gone abroad with his master had been serving with the Dutch, and had made some prize money. Learning on the peace that a small inheritance in Worcestershire had fallen to the family, they had returned, and found from Lady Blythedale that the brother's daughter was supposed to be alive somewhere near Bristol. She had a right to half, and being honourable men, they had set out in search of her, bringing letters from the lady to Mr. Henshaw, whose house was still a centre of inquiry for persons in the Cavalier interest. There, of course, they had discovered Emlyn; and Master Gaythorn proceeded to say that it had been decided that the estate should not be broken up, but that his son should at once wed her and unite their claims.

"But, sir," exclaimed Patience, "she is troth plight to my brother."

"So she told me, but likewise that he is a broken man and sickly, and had offered to restore her pledge."

Patience could not deny it, though she felt hotly indignant.

"She charged me to give it back to you," added the uncle; "and to bid you tell the young man that we are beholden to you both; but that since the young folk are to be wedded to-morrow morn, and then to set forth for Worcestershire, there is no time for leave-takings."

"I do not wonder!" exclaimed Patience, "that she has no face to see us. She that has been like a child or a sister to us, to leave us thus! O my brother!"

"Come, come, my good woman, best not make a pother." Poor Patience's homely garb and hard-worked looks shewed little of the yeoman class to which she belonged. "You've done your duty by the maid and here's the best I have to make it up."

Patience could not bring herself to take the bag, and he dropped it into her basket "I am sorry for the young man, your brother, but he knew better than to think to wed her as he is. And 'tis better for all there should be no women's tears and foolishness over it."

"Is she willing?" Patience could not but ask.

"Willing?" Both men laughed. "Aye, what lass is not willing to take a fine, strapping husband, and be a landed dame? She gave the token back of her own free will, eh, Humfrey; and what did she bid us say?"

"Her loving greetings to—What were their Puritanical names?" said the son contemptuously. "Aye, and that she pitied the poor clown down there, but knew he would be glad of what was best for her."

"So farewell, good mistress," said Master Gaythorn, and off they clanked together; and Patience, looking after them, could entirely believe that the handsome buff coat, fringed belt, high boots, and jauntily cocked hat would have driven out the thought of Stead in his best days. And now that he was bent, crippled, weak, helpless,—"and all through her, what hope was then," thought Patience, "yet if she had loved him, or there had been any truth in her, she could have wedded him now, and he would have been at ease through life! A little adder at our hearth! We are well quit of her, if he will but think so, but how shall I ever tell him?"

She did not rush in with the tidings but came home slowly, drearily, so that Stead, who was sitting outside by the door, peeling rushes, gathered that something was amiss, and soon wormed it out of her, while her tears dropped fast for him. Still, as ever, he spoke little. He said her uncle was right in sparing tears and farewells, no doubt reserving to himself the belief that it was against her will. And when Patience could not help declaring that the girl might have made him share her prosperity, he said, "I'm past looking after her lands. Her uncle would say so. 'Tis his doing; I am glad of what is best for my darling as was. There's an end of it, Patience—joy and grief. And I thank God that the child is safely cared for at last."

He tried to be as usual, but he was very ill that night.

Patience found the money in her basket. She hated it and put it aside, and it was only some time after that she was constrained to use it, only then telling Stead whence it came, when he could endure to hear that the uncle had done his best to be just.

CHAPTER XXIII

FULFILMENT

"My spirit heats her mortal bars,
  As down dark tides the glory glides,
  And mingles with the stars."
                TENNYSON.

The year 1660 had come, and in the autumn, just as harvest was over, and the trees on the slopes were taking tints of red, yellow, and brown, an elderly clergyman, staff in hand, came slowly up the long lane leading to Elmwood, whence he had been carried, bound to his horse, seventeen years before.

He had not suffered as much as some of his fellow priests. After a term of imprisonment in London, he had been transported to the plantations, namely, the American settlements, and had fallen in with friends, who took him to Virginia. This was chiefly colonized by people attached to the Church, who made him welcome, and he had ministered among them till the news arrived of the Restoration of Charles II, and likewise that the lawful incumbents of benefices, who had been driven out, were reinstated by Act of Parliament. Mr. Holworth's Virginian friends would gladly have kept him with them, but he felt that his duty was to his original flock, and set out at once for England, landing at Bristol. There, however, he waited, like the courteous man he was, to hold communication with his people, till he had written to Mr. Elmwood, and made arrangements with him and Master Woodley.

They were grieved, but they were both men who had a great respect for law and parliament, so they made no difficulties. Mr. and Mrs. Woodley retired to the hall and left the parsonage vacant, after the minister had preached a farewell sermon in the church which made everyone cry, for he was a good man and had made himself loved, and there were very few in the parish who could understand that difference between the true Church and a body without bishops. Mr. Holworth had in the meantime gone to Wells to see his own Bishop Piers, an old man of eighty-six, and it was from thence that he was now returning. He had not chosen to enter his parish till the intruded minister had resigned the charge, but he had been somewhat disappointed that none of his old flock, not even any Kentons, who had so much in charge, had come in to see him. He now arrived in this quiet way, thinking that it would not be delicate to the feelings of the squire and ex-minister to let the people get up any signs of joy or ring the bells, if they were so inclined. Indeed, he was much afraid from what he had been able to learn that it would be only the rougher sort, who hated Puritan strictness and wanted sport and revelry, who would give him an eager welcome.

So he first went quietly up to the church, which he found full of benches and pews, with the Altar table in the middle of the nave, and the squire's comfortable cushioned seat at the east end. He knelt on the step for a long time, then made a brief visit to his own house, where the garden was in beautiful order, but only a room or two were furnished with goods he had bought from the Woodleys, and these were in charge of a servant he had hired at Bristol.

Thence the old man went out into the village, and his first halt was at the forge, where Blane, who had grown a great deal stouter and more grizzled, started at sight of his square cap.

"Eh! but 'tis the old minister! You have come in quietly, sir! I am afraid your reverence has but a sorry welcome."

"I do not wonder you are grieved to part with Master Woodley."

"Well, sir, he be a good man and a powerful preacher, though no doubt your reverence has the best right, and for one, I'm right glad to see an old face again. We would have rung the bells if we had known you were coming."

"That would have been hard on Master Woodley. I am only glad they are not melted. But how is it with all my old friends, Harry? Poor Sir George writ me that old clerk North died of grief of the rifling of the church; and that John Kenton had been killed by some stragglers. What became of his children?"

"That eldest lad went off to the Parliament army, and came swaggering here in his buff coat and boots like my Lord Protector himself, they say he has got a castle and lands in Ireland. Men must be scarce, say I, if they have had to make a gentleman of Jeph Kenton."

"And the rest?"

"Well, sir, I'm afraid that poor lad, Stead, is in poor plight. You mind, he was always a still, steady, hard-working lad, and when his father was killed, and his house burnt, and his brother ran away, the way he and his sister turned to was just wonderful. They went to live in an old hut in the gulley down there, and they have made the place so tidy as it does your heart good to look at it. They bred up the young ones, and the younger girl is well married to one of the Squire's folks, and everyone respected them. But, as ill-luck would have it, some robbers from Bristol seem to have got scent of their savings. Some said that the Communion Cup was hid somewhere there."

Mr. Holworth made an anxious sound of interrogation.

"Well, I did see the corporal, when the Parliament soldiers were at Bristol, flog Stead shamefully to know where it was, and never get a word out of him, whether or no; and as he was a boy who would never tell a lie, it stands to reason he knew where they were."

"But how did anyone guess at his knowing?" asked Mr. Holworth.

"His brother might have thought it likely, poor John being thick with your reverence," said Blane. "After that I thought, myself, that he ought to give them up to Master Woodley, if so be he had them; but I could never get a hint from him. The talk went that old Dr. Eales, you mind him, sir, before he died, came out and held a prelatist service, begging your pardon, sir, and that the things were used. Stead got into trouble with Squire about it."

"But the robbers, how was that? You said he was hurt!"

"Sore hurt, sir; and he has never got the better of it, though 'tis nigh upon four years ago. There was a slip of a wench he picked up as a child after the fight by Luck's mill, and bred up; a fair lass she grew up to look on, but a light-headed one. She went to service at Bristol, and poor Stead was troth plight to her, hoped to save and build up the house again, never knowing, not he, poor rogue, of her goings on with the sailors and all the roistering lads about her master's house. 'Tis my belief she put those rascals on the track, whether she meant it or not. Stead made what defence he could, stood up like a man against the odds, three to one, and got a shot in the side, so that he was like to die then. Better for him, mayhap, if he had at once, for it has been nought but a lingering ever since, never able to do a day's work, though that wench, Patience, and the young lad, Ben, have fought it out wonderfully. That I will say."

Mr. Holworth had tears in his eyes, and trembled with emotion.

"The dear lad," he said. "Where is he? I must go and see him."

"He bides in the gulley, sir; he has been there ever since the farm-house was burnt."

Ere long Mr. Holworth was on his way to the gulley. What had been only a glade reaching from rock to stream, hidden in copsewood, was now an open space trodden by cattle, with the actual straw-yard more in the rear, but with a goat tethered on it and poultry running about. It was a sunny afternoon, and in a wooden chair placed so as to catch the warmth, with feet on a stool, sat, knitting, a figure that Mr. Holworth at first thought was that of an aged man; but as he emerged from the wood, and the big dog sprang up and barked, there was a looking up, an instant silencing of the dog, a rising with manifest effort, a doffing of the broad-brimmed hat, and the clergyman beheld what seemed to him his old Churchwarden's face, only in the deadly pallor of long-continued illness, and with the most intense, unspeakable look of happiness and welcome afterwards irradiating it, a look that in after years always came before Mr. Holworth with the "Nunc dimittis."

Dropping the knitting, and holding by the chair, he stood trembling and quivering with gladness, while, summoned by the dog's bark, Patience, pail in hand, appeared on one side, and Ben, tall and slight, with his flail, on the other.

"My dear lad," was all Mr. Holworth could say, as he took the thin, blanched hand, put his arm round the shoulders, and reseated Stead, still speechless with joy. Patience, curtseying low, came up anxiously, showing the same honest face as of old, though work and anxiety had traced their lines on the sun-burnt complexion, and Ben stood blushing, and showing his keener, more cultivated face, as the stranger turned to greet them so as to give Steadfast time to recover himself.

"Oh! sir, but we are glad to see your reverence," cried Patience. "Will you go in, or sit by Stead? Ben, fetch a chair."

"And is this fine strapping fellow, the sickly babe that you were never to rear, Patience?"

"God has been very good to us, sir," said Patience.

"And this is best of all," said Stead, recovering breath and speech. "I thank Him that I have lived to see this day! It is all safe, sir."

"And you, you faithful guardian, you have suffered for it."

If it had not been for Blane's partial revelations, Mr. Holworth never would have extracted the full story of how for that sacred trust, Steadfast Kenton had endured threats and pain, and had foregone ease, prosperity, latterly happiness, and how finally it had cost him health, nay life itself, for he was as surely dying of the buccaneer's pistol shot, as though he had been slain on the spot.

Long illness, with all the thought and reflection it had brought, had so far changed and refined Stead that his awkward bashfulness and lack of words had passed from him, and when he saw the clergyman overcome with emotion at the thought of all he had undergone he said,

"Never heed it, your reverence, it has come to be all joy to me to have had a little to bear for the Master! 'Tis hard on Patience and Ben, but they are very good to me; and being sick gives time for such comforts as God sends me. It is more than all I could have had here."

"I am sure of that, my dear boy. I was not grieving that I gave you the trust, but thinking what a blessed thing it is to have kept it thus faithfully."

Two Sundays later, the Feast was again meetly spread in Elmwood Church, the Altar restored to its place, and all as reverently arranged as it could yet be among the broken carved work.

In some respects it was a mournful service, few there were who after the lapse of seventeen years even remembered the outlines of the old forms; and the younger people knew not when to kneel or stand. There were few who could read, and even for those who could there were only four Prayer-books in the church, the clergyman's, the clerk's, the Kentons', and one discovered by an old Elmwood servant. The Squire's family came not; Goody Grace was dead, and though Rusha tried to instruct her husband and her little girl, she herself was much at a loss.

To Mr. Holworth it was almost like that rededication of the Temple when the old men wept at the thought of the glory of the former house, but there were some on whom his eye rested with joy and peace. There were Blane and his wife, good and faithful though ignorant; there were the old miller and his son, who had come all that distance since there had as yet been no restoration in their church, and the goings on of Original-Sin Hopkins and his friends had thoroughly disgusted them, and made the old man yearn towards the church of his youth, and there was the little group of three, the toil-worn but sweet-faced sister, calm and restful, though watchful; the tall youth with thoughtful, earnest, awe-struck face, come for his first Communion, for which through those many years he had been taught to pray and long, and between them the wasted form and wan features lighted up with that wonderful radiance that had come on them with the sense that the trust was fulfilled, only it was brighter, calmer, higher, than even at the greeting of the vicar. Did Steadfast see only the burnished gold of the Chalice and paten he had guarded for seventeen years at the cost of toil, danger, suffering, love, and life itself? Did he not see and feel far beyond those outward visible signs in which others, who had not yet endured to the end, could only as yet put their trust by faith?

Mr. Holworth, as he stood over him and saw the upturned eye, was sure it was so. No doubt indeed Ben thought so too, but poor imaginative Ben had somehow fancied it would be with his brother as with the King who guarded that other sacred Cup, and when all was over, was quite disappointed that Stead needed his strong arm as much as ever, nay more, for on coming out into the air and sunshine a faintness and exhaustion came on, and they had to rest him in the porch before he could move.

"O Stead, I thought it would have healed you," the lad said.

Stead slightly smiled. "Healed? I shall soon be healed altogether, Ben," he said. He had with great difficulty and very slowly walked to church, and Mr. Holworth wished him to come and rest at the Vicarage, but he was very anxious to get home, and after he had taken a little food, Andrew Luck offered to share with Ben and Rusha's husband the carrying him back between them on an elbow chair.

This pleased him, and he looked up to Andrew and said, "You are in the same mind as long ago?"

"I never found anyone else I could lay my mind to, since my poor Kitty," said Andrew.

"She will come to you—soon," said Stead. "She'll have a sore heart, but you will be good to her."

"That I will. And little Bess and Kate shall come and tell her how they want her."

Stead smiled and his lips moved in thankfulness.

"And if Ben would come with her," added Andrew, "I'd be a brother to him."

"Parson wants Ben," said Stead. "He says he can make a scholar of him, and maybe a parson, and it will not be so lonesome in the vicarage."

"And your farm?"

"Rusha and her man take that. They have saved enough to build the house. Yes, all is well. It is great peace and thankfulness."

Patience returned with the cushions she had borrowed and they brought Steadfast home, very much exhausted, and not speaking all the way. Perhaps the unusual motion and exertion had made the bullet change its place, for he hardly uttered another word, and that night, as he had said to Ben, he was healed for ever of all his ills.

The funeral sermon that Mr. Holworth preached the next Sunday, was on the text so dear to all the loyal hearts who remembered the White King's coronation text—

"Be thou faithful unto death, and I will give thee a crown of life."

THE END.

CPSIA information can be obtained
at www.ICGtesting.com
Printed in the USA
BVHW082058030223
657845BV00003B/84

9 789395 675482